PRAISE FOR WILDERNESS WARS

Wilderness Wars slow-builds menace from its nail-biting opening to its stunning apocalyptic climax. This is a golden eagle of a book—it grabs you in its talons and won't let go. A thought-provoking and often frightening study of what happens when you mess with Nature and Nature decides to fight back. And how faith, family and friendship can forge the right path.

Olivia Levez

Author of *The Island* and *The Circus*

To Frank,

BARBARA HENDERSON

Go wild!

WILDERNESS WARS

Barbara Henderson

x

pokey
hat

First published in 2018 by Pokey Hat

Pokey Hat is an imprint of Cranachan Publishing Limited

ISBN: 978-1-911279-34-1
eISBN: 978-1-911279-35-8

Cover Illustration: Seascape
© shutterstock.com / Vadym Prokhorenko

www.cranachanpublishing.co.uk

@cranachanbooks

cranachan

For my wonderful friend Sandra, wildlife artist and first reader of this manuscript.

CHAPTER ONE

RAGE

There is a jolt, throwing me forward into my seatbelt.

The car has stopped.

Wading my way back to consciousness through several layers of sleep, I hear Dad's excited voice: 'That's it, that shape in the distance. Do you see it?'

I lean forward. Beside me, Struan rubs his eyes and does the same.

Still in a daze, I take it all in:

The wind, the leaden skies, the churning moody sea. The ferry, loaded high with supplies and building equipment, Dad shaking hands with his new team, the grey pier and the greyer waves…

And, far in the distance, a misty outline.

Skelsay.

Wilderness haven. Building-site. Luxury-retreat-to-be.

And now, home.

'Aha,' exclaims Mum, pointing to a small group of people standing around in high-visibility raincoats on the deck of the ferry. 'There they are!'

Struan stretches and runs his fingers through his ginger mop of hair. 'Who?'

'Dad's workforce and their families. Come on, let's do this, kids!' She pulls her coat around her neck more closely, leans back to unclip Izzy from her car seat, and wriggles out with my baby sister clutched to her hip. Struan and I follow.

'Will Snarl be all right in the car, Mum?' my little brother wants to know.

'Of course he will; he's a hamster. He's been perfectly fine in his cage for all these hours, and a couple more won't bother him.'

We make our way past Dad who is patting a pot-bellied man on the back and laughing.

'Let's get on the boat, and you can have your packed lunch, right? It'll take them a while to load all our containers and to get the cars and diggers on. It'll be a tight squeeze.'

Even while she is speaking, Mum drinks in the view: the wide skies, the windborne bird-shapes in the distance, winging across the waves which come crashing in like clockwork. I can tell she is framing in her mind; she's a natural artist; it's the way her mind works. Watching her makes *me* see the splendour of it, too, and I breathe a little deeper. With every step across the narrow walkway towards the boat, my excitement grows. We're going. We're finally going.

It's only for a year—maybe two at most if there are problems with the construction. Either way, all my friends are still going to be there when I get back. And it is cool, living on an uninhabited island. Hang on; it's probably not uninhabited anymore, now that all of us are going to be there, is it? Oh, I don't know…

I'm so absorbed by all of these thoughts that, unlike my little brother, I don't even complain when Mum hands me an egg sandwich.

On the ferry deck itself stand five women and seven or eight children. I scan the faces.

Then I scan them *again*.

Don't tell me…

I look around, desperately. No, I haven't missed anybody!

But Dad said there'd be another…

'DAD!' I yell.

An hour later, we are rocked from side to side with the ferry's motion. My father has finally condescended to talk to me, but he is pretty unrepentant.

'Dad, you *promised* me there'd be another girl my age!' I'm quietly sizzling with rage, since I can't exactly shriek in a tiny ferry lounge where a handful of damp strangers are being polite to one another.

'Look, Em, I didn't think it would matter that much.'

I sulk in silence, sipping tea from a nameless builder's flask. I hate sweet, milky tea, but it's the only drink on offer. It's hot. Better than nothing.

Dad tries again: 'It's not as if I haven't had other things on my mind, you know. It's not all about you, Em!'

I turn my face away.

'Very well. I'll leave you to it,' mutters Dad and disappears up the metal stairs to the deck, leaving me to my thoughts.

You let me down, Dad! Badly.

I freeze my frown and stare into the distance where the Isle of Harris shrinks further away with every minute. The smaller Isle of Taransay glides by. Just then, the ferry gives an enormous jolt as it changes direction and more than half of the sickly, now lukewarm, cup of death lands right in my lap. I roll my eyes and groan. *Wonderful! Can this day get any worse?*

Turns out, it can.

CHAPTER TWO

BIRDS

The door squeaks open and a whole group of new people piles in: the pot-belly guy with the moustache, a small round woman with frizzy hair, a thin boy with glasses and the haircut from hell, another young couple and a baby.

Quickly, I grab my jacket and throw it over my steaming lap. Another man walks in now, wearing corduroy trousers and a scuffed tweed jacket. *Wonder who that is. He doesn't look like an architect. Dad said one of them would visit quite early on, but I don't think...*

'Hey!'

I feel a nudge to my side. The boy with the glasses has sat down beside me and I am forced to really look at him: the mop of blond hair, the baggy jeans and the hole in the sleeve of his home-knit jumper.

Turning away, I pretend to focus on the view, even though I can barely make anything out through the uniform grey of the windowpane.

The truth is: I feel betrayed. Snippets of conversations around the dinner table back in Glasgow echo in my memory:

How do you fancy a wee stint on an island?

Some of the others are bringing their families, Karen. Head Office say they might even take care of schooling to keep the workforce consistent.

Oh, and Em, I'm sure the site manager has a daughter about your age.

What a mug I am, to count on anything Dad says. He didn't even bother to ask or check.

The door flies open again and a band of younger kids —led by Struan, surprise, surprise—explodes into the room. He holds on to the back-rests of the seats on both sides as he makes his way up the small aisle, followed by two girls and another three boys. They could be anything between five and ten.

'I'm Zac, by the way,' says the boy beside me as if he hasn't realised how awkward I'm being.

'Em,' I reply monosyllabically when Struan interrupts, his eyes bright.

'Yeah, right, everybody, this is Em. She's my big sister. She's twelve. Yep, that's about all I can say about her.'

This meets with small-kid giggles.

'Haha! You're so funny,' I answer, but Struan has no sarcasm-radar.

'Honestly, Em, you should come up and eat lunch out

on deck! The waves are mental and Izzy's fallen asleep so Mum's staying by the car with her. She'd never let us, so now's your only chance! It's wicked! Mikey here's just been sick and I've seen three seals already! Come on!'

Struan's group clamber up the steep metal stair again, a boy with a greenish tinge stumbling up at the rear.

Zac rises and looks at me. I'd almost forgotten he was there. 'I'm going to check out those seals. You coming?'

I roll my eyes at him, even though it's Dad I'm angry with. 'Oh, fine then! Hang on.'

My voice sounds as if, somehow, I'm doing him a great favour, but if he thinks I'm a stuck-up cow, he doesn't show it.

I tie my jacket around my waist to hide the spill, pour what's left in the cup into a dried-up plant pot and stretch. On the way up, I have to squeeze past Dad. I don't even want to look at him.

On deck, people stand side by side along the railing, pointing at the looming grey shape in the mist. A rounded, twisted hill, and what looks like trees sheltered beneath it. Rocky, grassy cliffs and the bright glow of a shingle beach just visible around the left corner. Skelsay, 'Isle of Shells'.

The island that will be home to us all.

'There!' shouts Zac beside me, zipping up his green parka.

'What?'

'Look!'

He points. Right enough, a dark head moves up and down in the waves, followed by another a little to the left.

'I've seen seals before,' I lie in a bored voice. I hate myself when I'm like this, but I just can't help it. Zac shrugs and walks further along to the bow to get a closer look. For a few seconds he fumbles in his coat pocket for something. Then he pulls out a minuscule pair of binoculars and looks out to sea.

I sniff to show how little I care about being ignored and sink onto a bench to unwrap my sandwich.

And that's when it happens.

I can't say what, apart from the fact that the air is suddenly filled with shrieks, feathers and, above all, pain.

Struan screams as a gull pecks him hard on the top of his head. I hit out at everything and anything around my head—wings, feet, beaks and, I'm sure of it—Zac—on a couple of occasions.

And suddenly, Dad is there, roaring louder than I'd have ever believed him capable, ripping off his coat and using it to wave the birds away, but still they keep on coming. Three of them swoop towards his head at once and he drops his coat, hitting out with his bare fists instead, but a gash has appeared on his cheek by the time they soar again.

'Down!' I yell, seizing Struan by the scruff of his neck and stumbling towards the door to the stairs. 'Get down there!' *He's my brother; he's only eight,* is all I can think.

The younger children disappear through one by one while Zac, Dad and I shield the doorway for them as best we can. Feathery wings whip at our faces and one gull's hooked beak pecks relentlessly at my father's leg. He brings his fist down on it and the bird flutters to the floor before retreating, shaking its head.

Zac has lost his balance and staggers backwards towards the low railing on the slippery deck. *NO!* Dad recognises the danger too and both of us lunge forward. We clutch at Zac's parka to stop him sliding overboard while another gull keeps dive-bombing us from above. With an effort, we pull Zac to his feet, but it's hard: the boy thrashes out blindly with his eyes shut tight, his glasses askew. Bundling him towards safety below deck, I yell, wave my hands; try to whack the sky-brutes with my jacket, but as soon as we edge backwards towards the doorway, the attack abates.

The shadow of a huge bird appears and brushes over us again. All we can do is gape at one another, bewildered. The shadow returns, smaller this time, but we still duck. We see it fly past in the distance one more time before it is swallowed up by cloud or waves, I don't know which.

'Whoa!' croaks Zac.

Shivering, I turn back towards the stairs. Mum's voice carries up from the lounge now, no doubt trying to calm Struan down. Along the length of the boat, I catch a glimpse of our ever-shifting trail on the water, writhing white on the dark expanse of the Atlantic as Harris vanishes from view.

I look again.

Bobbing seal heads, like the two ahead.

Only now it's hundreds. *Hundreds*, with their smooth skin reflecting the ripples in the water, and their black eyes prying. Watching. Waiting.

Ahead in the gathering cloud, the towering shape of Skelsay threatens to swallow us whole.

CHAPTER THREE

HOME

We arrive in the late afternoon, but the team is prepared. Huge floodlights are quickly set up and for the first time, we see our 'village': the neat row of portacabins nestling by the newly completed pier. The slope rises behind the settlement, towards a sheltered wooded dell, protected from the wind. Probably the only reason trees can grow out here at all. Below it, a dirt track leads around the coast to the smaller second site as the hill rises inland. It's so strange; our little pop-up village—it hardly seems real.

'Home sweet home,' mumbles Mum beside me, her short dark hair blown into a windswept mess. Izzy is wrapped in so many layers, she barely looks human.

'Quick then, guys, let's move before it gets too dark,' urges Dad and the crane rolls down the ramp, a long chain dangling from its point.

'Best if you all watch from land,' shouts the moustache man called Harvey, breaking our spell. We shuffle down toff the boat ahead of the other vehicles.

'Head to that hut over there, the one for the building supplies. Door should be open,' hollers Dad over the wind and Mum, carrying Izzy on her hip, leads the way. I shrug and follow while the workers spread out like ants.

We congregate in the largest cabin which reminds me a little of my aunt and uncle's caravan, only much bigger and without any furniture. Stacks of paper and a handful of boxes are already piled up by the door and below the window. To my surprise, the Tweed-jacket-man follows.

'Who is that guy?' I mouth to Zac who has ended up beside me again. 'He doesn't really look like the architect type.'

Zac grins. 'That's because he's not an architect.' His grey eyes meet mine properly for the first time.

'How do you know?'

'I asked him,' he shrugs.

I raise my eyebrows as high as I can.

'And?'

'He's our teacher. He's called Mr Johnston.'

Our teacher? I don't know why, but it never occurred to me that there would be an actual person employed to teach us; I expected it to be more of a home-schooling thing. Now I feel completely stupid. Thankfully, nobody sees my stunned expression as a piercing yell cuts through the air outside.

'GO!'

We watch as the crane lifts the first container high above the crashing waves, swinging gently sideways. Slowly, the metal crate is deposited on the square of compressed mud and our packed little portacabin erupts into claps and cheers.

I remember packing our own container, back in Glasgow a million zillion light years from this windswept coast. Four mattresses to go on the wall-mounted foldaway beds, a small futon, a folding table and chairs, a box of clothes for now, a box of clothes one size up for us to grow into, books, games, all Mum's painting stuff... The list is endless. Life as we know it is in that box. I placed the goodbye-card that my school friends made me into it myself, and all the old photos of when Struan and I were babies. My Bluetooth speakers, my weaving frame. And the mystery birthday present from Gran and Grandad, wrapped and ready for when I turn thirteen in the autumn. Only the last-minute stuff went into the car. Plus Struan's stupid hamster of course.

'Here goes!' says Mum. Her voice catches slightly as container 19 rises into the air above the spray. Is it just me or do the waves reach higher, try harder than before? I peek at Mum, but her eyes are glued to our boxed-up metal world, dangling on that chain. The crane sways and the weight of the crate rocks the vehicle. I hear a sharp intake of breath, but with an audible thud, our container lands safely beside the first.

'Thank goodness!' groans Mum, but the knuckles on her fist are still white.

'Next!' sounds the same sharp yell outside.

'They know what they are doing. Not too long now. Here's a flask of tea. Anyone?' A young woman called Petra with a blonde ponytail waves a stack of paper cups above her head. 'And there are biscuits, too.'

At this, we flutter towards her like moths to light, chatting or laughing nervously. The two babies crawl around the empty floor and the meeting and greeting continues, instigated by the frizzy-haired woman. I've worked out that she is Zac's mother and called Muriel. Suddenly, a young woman gives an involuntary shriek and points.

There is a stampede back to the window, with plenty of elbowing each other as we go. The level of shouting outside even rises above the howling wind. I see what they mean.

The waves seem to be launching themselves at container 7, which is spinning wildly from side to side. The woman operating the crane is struggling to maintain control over the vehicle. I only catch glimpses of her, in between sprays of water washing across her windscreen. She attempts to turn the crane, but the metal container is forced towards her by a strong and erratic gust.

It swings back again, as if in slow motion.

Towards the ferry.

Into the ferry bow.

The impact snaps the chain like thread...

And container 7 plummets downwards with a splash, hovers on the surface of the sea for a moment, then sinks out of sight, swallowed up by the churning waters.

There is silence in the cabin. All eyes turn to Zac and his frizzy-haired mother.

CHAPTER FOUR

SECRETS

I'm so cold. How can anyone be expected to sleep like this, with the racket of the sea? The wind hammers on the door with threats unknown, while inside, deep breathing from strangers sounds out all around. We lie on the hard floor of the cabin, sandwiched together for warmth and covered by every jacket, sleeping-bag, blanket and tablecloth we could salvage before dark. Shame we couldn't get to the mattresses. Dad took charge, abandoning the unloading. The ferry secured, both tied and anchored, there is no choice but to wait out the storm.

It's all a bit much. Two days ago, I left behind the garden flat in Glasgow where I've spent my whole life. Here I am now, sleeping in a corrugated iron shed in the middle of nowhere.

There is some comfort in numbers, I suppose. I'm glad Mum is beside me.

The men have volunteered to sleep on the ferry,

along with the teacher—Mr Johnston—and the crane-lady. I wish they'd taken the hamster cage with them, but Struan insisted on having Snarl in here, and that annoying hamster wheel is whirring every few seconds. Despite it all, I'm gradually lulled to sleep by the muffled sobs of Muriel, who has curled herself up in the corner by the door.

The next morning, I feel as if I've woken in a dream. Sunrays bathe the tired sleepers on the floor in yellow, burnt orange and gold as sea birds circle across the window and cast their graceful shadows over us.

I sit up and blink in the bright light. Dad's team have already begun their work: a neat row of metal crates sits beside ours on dry land and another is heaved and dropped beside the rest in a smooth manoeuvre executed by the crane operator—the same woman. I pull myself up on my knees and narrow my eyes for a closer look. She looks sort of middle-aged, with wavy reddish-brown hair pulled into a messy bun. She wears the same blue overalls as the rest of them.

'Morning,' whispers Mum beside me with a careful eye on Izzy who is stirring at her feet. 'Sleep OK?'

'Hmmm.'

Her eyes follow mine. 'I asked your Dad about that woman, by the way. She's called Erica. Quite experienced from what he says. She's worked all over the world, leading building projects for some charity—I forget which.'

I nod again, but my mind has long abandoned this conversation.

The door opens and Harvey sticks his head round.

'Morning. Everything is unloaded, so we need to get ourselves set up as best as we can.' It seems as if he wanted to say something else, but he just swallows and squeezes the shoulder of the frizzy-haired woman as he passes, adding: 'Meeting in an hour by the pier.'

Zac—where did *he* come from?—appears at my side: 'That was my Dad.'

I wonder what they're going to do. Like a slow-motion film, I imagine their container, ten or twenty metres below the surface, resting on the seabed and being rocked back and forth by the tide until it's wedged firmly into its new home. Zac seems to read my mind and grimaces.

'We're just going to have to improvise, I suppose.'

He makes it sound like an adventure somehow, but I'm sure that's not how his mother sees it. Her face is swollen and red and there are dark shadows under her eyes.

The day is spent assigning portacabins to each family and individual. Ours is beside Petra and Steve's at the edge of the settlement, sheltered by a single windswept tree which has somehow grown much taller than any others on the island.

It is only in the daylight that I realise that some of the longer huts consist of individual pods, and that some large containers hold the belongings of several individuals. My Mum organises a collection, so that Zac's family can begin to furnish their space, even just a little. It is agreed that when the architect makes his initial visit tomorrow, Muriel will go back with him by helicopter and make arrangements.

'Don't worry about money,' Dad says, patting her on the back awkwardly. 'We're insured and the company will pay out—I'll make sure of that.'

I've hardly seen Struan all day. He's been outside, discovering his new territory while I try to help Mum and find my own feet in the strange new world of our cabin. I split my time between unpacking the huge crate with Mum and playing with Izzy on the shingle beach by the pier. Towards evening I begin sorting out the small compartment that is now my room. I can hear every word, whisper and wobble through the thin metal walls, but the view from the window more than makes up for it.

So here I am on Skelsay, and here I'll remain until the project's done.

I allow my mind to wander and imagine.

I'll be a couple of years older and the waves will still

bear down on the pier. Only there'll be a top-of-the-range golf course then, and a ten-storey luxury hotel with heated pools and roof Jacuzzis for the use of the lucky guests who can afford the Saltire Suites at the top of each tower. The gym will look out over the Atlantic with its whales and dolphins. A funicular railway will take guests up the Ben. The hill does have some other unpronounceable name, probably Gaelic, but 'the Ben' does it for me; Dad's been talking about it for months. I picture the restaurant at the top, made entirely of glass, with 360° views all round. My head's spinning, even thinking about it.

Specialists will come and go, but the core workforce… well, that's us. Dad and his people.

I'm distracted by creaking and scraping noises against the surface above my fold-down bed.

'Struan!'

'What?' comes the voice through the wall. It should be muffled, but of course it isn't—just a tad metallic.

'Shut up.'

'I'm doing nothing!'

'So what's the creaking?'

'Just Blu Tack. I'm putting my posters up!'

I groan. This doesn't bear thinking about. 'I can hear everything, Struan!'

'I know! I can hear you, too. Only I'm not whingeing about it.'

'Shut up, Struan!'

'You're repeating yourself, Em! Think of something new!'

I nearly say 'shut up' again but catch myself just in time and bang hard on the wall. Struan answers with a burp to which—of course—I have no reply.

'You're revolting!'

His head pokes around the corner of my door.

'I know!' His grin displays more gaps than teeth.

I leave in mock disgust, giving him a wee tickle on the way past, and wander through to the kitchen. Mum is making a third—noisy—attempt to force our stack of pots and pans into the narrow cupboard above the two-ring gas cooker.

'Where's the food going to go?' I ask and wrinkle my forehead. *There are two small cupboards. We are a family of five. Go figure.*

'The Storehouse,' mumbles Mum absent-mindedly and nods to a blue wooden shed across the square of flattened mud. 'We'll all use it and most of the food supplies are kept there. Next supply boat comes in a week.'

I wander around the kitchen, the fold-down table, the folding chairs and the collapsible high chair. Then I do it again.

There's NO room to pace!

'Can I help?' I ask. After all, there's only so long you

can spend unpacking a box and putting three posters on the wall. Mum wipes a sweaty strand of hair from her forehead. 'That'd be great, Em. Let me see... Dad's going to have his office in there...'

'I thought that was a cupboard!'

Mum ignores me and points to a box of folders. 'All the stuff in those boxes has to go on the shelves in there. Could you flatten the empty ones straight after and take them to the recycling container, please? We need to save some room in here. Thanks, Em. TURN THAT DOWN, STRUAN!'

'It's on the lowest setting already!' bellows Struan's voice through the wall.

'Use headphones then!'

I grin as I carry the files into Dad's minuscule office. I quite like making things look organised, especially when I've nothing better to do.

Methodically, I tie back my mane of curly brown hair and begin, setting folders out in order of colour and then size. Dad's pretty meticulous when it comes to paperwork. I balance the half-empty second box on the desk and stretch to pin the poster of the artist's impression up above.

There, just as it was in Glasgow.

I can't resist looking at the painting again. Beneath the swirly title, 'Skelsay Skies Resort', the sun is shining on the turquoise sea. Dolphins leap against the sunset, and the gleaming buildings are filled with happy and contented people, none of whom are old or overweight—or children, for that matter. The small group of golfers on the immaculately groomed green are raising their hands in celebration, at a particularly good shot, I imagine.

It feels so unreal, so mad, to think that this wild island could soon look like this.

I don't know how I do it, but somehow, while bending to the side to fix the edges of the picture, I knock the remaining box to the floor with a thud. Papers sail in all directions. I hold my breath. *Has Mum heard?*

Stupid question. She can probably hear me breathe in here.

'You all right, Em?' comes her voice through the thin wall, but she's obviously not concerned enough to come through and check.

'Fine! Sorry.'

I begin to gather the papers I've dropped. Luckily, Dad doesn't keep many loose sheets, and most are properly filed. I leaf through the folders to make sure all is well when something catches my attention.

What's this doing in here?

Intrigued, I survey the article with colourful images of birds and animals along the top. I check the label of the folder: *Project Press Coverage.*

I take a closer look.

The headline reads:

Animals Under Threat: Luxury Development in the Outer Hebrides

Scotland on Sunday has received an open letter signed by a number of high-profile environment charities, raising concerns about a luxury leisure development planned on the currently uninhabited island of Skelsay, located north-east of St Kilda.

It claims the development risks destroying crucial habitats for the rare corncrake, a bird once common on the west coast of Scotland but now threatened by extinction. In addition, the small island has been home to breeding pairs of white-tailed sea eagles, golden eagles, as well as feral goats and red deer. The elusive pine marten and water vole are also said to be thriving on the island while its wide range of wild flowers is almost unmatched in Scotland.

When Skelsay was sold by its private owner Michael Ballantyne-Forsyth, the third Baron of the Isles, a decade ago, Prime Isles Development Ltd acquired the land. However, planning permission for the exclusive resort was only obtained last year.

'We are extremely disappointed that Scotland should put profit above protection of our cherished environment, much of which is what brings tourists to our shores. I hope that Parliament will reconsider its decision in the light of our evidence,' a spokesman for the Scottish Wildlife Trust said yesterday.

However, Dr Ian Pratt, project architect, responded: 'Planning permission has been granted and I resent the scare-mongering indulged in by the Wildlife Trust and others.

We intend to complement Skelsay's natural beauty with our development and, through it, will enable many more people to share in it. The project will create hundreds of permanent jobs in the Hebrides which—quite rightly—the Scottish Parliament has encouraged. I have nothing further to add.'

A legal attempt to block the plans, launched by the charities, was rejected last week. Construction is set to begin in the spring.

I'm so engrossed I don't even hear Struan tiptoe in.

'What's that?' he asks, and I jump.

While I recover, he looks over my shoulder. 'Are you snooping?'

'I suppose. Sort of,' I whisper back. 'You never know when a bit of secret knowledge may come in useful.'

A wide grin spreads over my brother's face until it reaches his ears.

He rubs his hands and makes himself comfortable.

'Tell me then.'

CHAPTER FIVE

SCHOOL

Dad and I are officially talking again. It's kind of awkward ignoring someone who is never further than eight metres away from you, wherever you are in the cabin. I lasted two days. I'm not proud of it, but there it is.

Of course he didn't apologise—Dad doesn't do "sorry"—but he's sort of trying to make an effort; I can tell. Mum shoots me this pleading look that she keeps in reserve to prod the deepest, darkest bits of my conscience, and my huff just hovers away.

I doubt Dad even notices the difference, truth be told; he's been so busy with the architect who arrived all by himself in a helicopter. What a snotty-nosed, stuck-up, slimy git that man is. I imagine he might be quite glamorous in London, but here he looks absolutely ridiculous, with that gelled-across-the-forehead hairdo and the geek-chic glasses.

Even Dad doesn't like him much if he's honest (which he isn't).

Dr Ian Pratt.

'His parents obviously couldn't spell...' suggests Struan as we wait for the school door to open the day after, watching the chopper fade into the distance. 'They meant to write "*I am a prat*". That's a good name for him!'

My brother's little band of disciples snigger with delight.

'Anyway, he's gone now; and good riddance!'

Zac's Mum is gone, too, of course, but it doesn't seem to get him down too much. I have decided that I can't blame him forever for not being a girl my age—after all, he's probably my best bet for a friend. And let's face it, I'm desperate.

Finally, the door creaks and we can set foot into the long portacabin at the edge of our 'village' at last. I've been in once before when we all got the tour, but this is it. The first day of normal routine on Skelsay.

Mr Johnston smiles as he motions for us to sit down and I glance around in wonder. He *has* been busy! Posters of animals and maps, achievement charts, sayings and quotes, photos and pin boards... there isn't a space on the wall that's empty. *Where on earth did he get the curtains?* And in the corner, there is a lit wood-burning stove with a gigantic basket of logs beside. Compared with the windy wet world we've just left behind, this is paradise!

Not that I am about to tell him that.

'Right. Let's sort you into learning groups. Emma and Zachary, you are going to be in this corner here...'

My luck's finally in! Right by the stove and the window overlooking the cove. Along the coast, the brightness of the coral beach glows beyond the machair, as if to spite the dark skies. I look at Zac whose eyes are already following some sort of huge bird circling high, high in the sky.

Struan protests loudly when he is told to sit by the door, and even *more* loudly when he doesn't get to sit beside Mikey or Tom. Instead, he has to make do with the much more sensible Gregor.

'None of these arrangements are permanent,' says Mr Johnston calmly, but Struan doesn't look in the least reassured. I cough to hide my chuckle. It is a welcome change to watch someone else torment my brother.

The morning passes quite pleasantly, with only reading and maths assessments and some sort of questionnaire to find out what sort of topics we've already covered at school. The sun shines through the window while the wind whistles down the chimney, stirring up fireworks of sparks only Zac and I can see. Life is good.

It's breezy, but we still go out at lunch. The wind plays swing-ball with my ponytail until I manage to fix my hood. Apparently, we're not allowed to climb down to the cove. Again, Struan protests vigorously, but the hillside above it is almost as good.

The afternoon is slightly less pleasant on account of a significant dent to my pride. Zac—who is nearly eight months younger than me—has scored higher marks than me in both maths and reading! I do my best to conceal my outrage, but he must have noticed anyway.

'Don't worry about it! Swings and roundabouts,' he says.

'What do you mean?'

'Just that you'll probably wipe the floor with me the next time we do a test. You weren't far behind anyway.'

'I'm not bothered!' I say and turn my back, toasting my face in the heat of the stove.

'Right, everyone. Have all of you finished? We are going to begin our first piece of writing which I'd like you to finish for homework. I'm aware that most of you don't know each other well yet, either, so the title is: *A personal response: Coming to Skelsay*. Think of it as a showcase, using your best vocabulary, your most convincing description, your most exciting storytelling, your most thoughtful reflection. Em and Zac, I'm of course expecting significantly more detail from you two.' Mr Johnston is still wearing the corduroys, twinned with a thick knitted jumper and a woolly scarf. Unbidden images of *I-am-a-prat* come into my mind and I sharpen my pencil while I regain control of my urge to laugh.

My personal response? Where on earth do I begin? I accidentally poke myself with my much-sharper-than-usual pencil as I cup my face in my hands and mull the last few days over in my mind. It's looking hopeful.

Disasters are great to write about. The gulls, the container, the fall-out with Dad.

Mr Johnston's going to *love* my essay, I think.

Sudden flurries of hailstones bombard the windows, replaced by gently falling flakes as I write and write and write.

'And? How was it?' asks Mum as we trudge in at three in the afternoon.

'Yeah…' I mumble, grateful to Struan for launching a lament which distracts my mother for a full ten minutes, while I escape to my room and try to get my head around what's bothering me. My fingers flick through the pages of my essay.

Get over it, Em. It's nothing. Everything is new, that's why you're feeling like this. Don't give it another thought.

Resolutely, I close my exercise book and vow to think of nothing sinister or threatening for the rest of the day. Anna and Catriona skip past the window, waving matching pink skipping ropes and I roll my eyes. Minutes later, Erica the crane woman walks past and heads towards the Ben.

Half an hour after that, the cliffs are dusted in white and I can barely see the pier in the distance.

Despite the weather the two diggers are still going. I

hear their noise as I run over to the storehouse to fetch more spaghetti for Mum; I hear it over Struan's whingeing as he has to clear the table and I'm still hearing it as I splash my face in the microscopic bathroom where my bum touches the door as I brush my teeth in front of the sink. The water is a brownish yellow, but it's surprising what you can get used to.

'Hey, Dad. How deep are they actually digging?'

'Just over two metres, but some of the ground is stonier than we thought. We've got to stay on schedule, though—we've already lost a couple of days.'

His face is healing up now, although I can still see bruises on his arm and his leg is bound to hurt. I think of the delay in getting here and of the time something got stuck in the digger's…whatever the claw-y bit is called. Erica ended up fixing it with twenty men looking on. Said she had to improvise in Africa all the time.

And we've only been here a week.

'Early days yet,' mumbles Dad. 'What are you thinking?'

'Nothing. Just school and stuff.'

'I'm glad it was all right. Zac seems nice enough.' Dad contorts his face into a grimace. *He knows he's let me down.* I mimic him and as we stare each other out in a manic grin, I realise: this is his apology.

'You could FaceTime Ellie tonight…' he suggests.

'If she's in.'

I fight it with all my might, but I know the signs. I'm welling up, thinking of my friends in Glasgow who still have each other—and me, stuck on this island with my brother and his gang, two pink Barbie-lovers, a couple of babies… and Zac. I need to change the subject before I start howling.

'By the way, Dad, you've got spaghetti in your beard.'

CHAPTER SIX

PRATT

I've decided school is all right. Mr Johnston is a bit weird, the way he stares you in the eye and doesn't look away, but other than that, he's fine. He's got a nice deep voice, like Dad. Not a whiney, squeaky voice like *I-am-a-prat*, for example…

We're all herded out of the building by Mr Johnston who seems to be in a mood for some reason. We wrap our jackets tightly around ourselves and stand on what we call 'the square'—the area of compacted mud between our huts and the storehouse.

'Brrhch!' exaggerates Struan and 'brrhch' echo another four little voices. Zac and I stand near the back, a little bit apart and glaring in different directions. I think of the stove, churning warm smoke into the sky, warming my seat on which I am not sitting.

Instead I'm standing here for this pointless, pointless exercise.

Mum and Izzy and Petra and baby Lena are already

here. Zac nods to Muriel, just back off the supply boat yesterday. Harvey is standing in the middle with Dad and the guys. Erica is looking over to us.

Mr Johnston has brightened up. And suddenly, there he is: Pratt, standing tall on the wooden platform Dad nailed together for him last night (under duress I think). The architect's hair is gelled up rather than across today, and he's wearing trousers and a jumper instead of the suit, but he still looks far too co-ordinated and clean.

He looks absurd, actually. He sounds ludicrous too.

'Well, hello there, team. I wanted to take this opportunity to speak to you all together as we embark on this exciting project. The 'Skelsay Skies' resort will be SPEC-TAC-ULAR!'

He waits, probably for applause. When none comes, he has no choice but to carry on.

'Like all bold and brave projects, Skelsay Skies has not been without controversy, but we have overcome every hurdle along the way, and now we're here, with the first stage well under way. Before your very eyes, it will rise up from the earth; a development which will be the talk of the architectural world, a place every man, woman and child will ache to visit…'

I hear a chortle but resist the temptation to turn and see who it is. We've been well warned. The wind keeps blowing his hair out of shape as he speaks, and he keeps trying to style it up again. I feel the beginnings of a chuckle, deep in my chest.

'You've all seen the artist's impression, but I've decided that—in order to have true ownership of this, the NEW Skelsay—you each need to have a copy of your own. The office has printed them beautifully and in colour. Put them up in your huts. Don't just look at them; *see* them. *See* the *amazing* thing you are all part of. And be proud.'

His fringe hovers horizontally, like a flag fluttering atop his narrow face. I hold my breath and bite my lip at the same time. *How much longer?*

'As you know, I will visit as frequently as my other commitments allow. I hope we are all going to get along very well.'

It takes us a second to work out that he has finally finished. Then Dad claps, slowly, and the rest of us join in. Mum and Petra have begun to amble back to the huts, probably to keep the babies warm.

'No wait!' the whiny voice squeals. 'Take your copies!' He produces a shiny cardboard box and opens the lid. 'If you could form an orderly queue, please...'

I exchange a look with Zac and it's over—the giggles claim us both. Dad frowns across, begging me not to embarrass him, but all I can do is press my lips together hard as my shoulders rock with suppressed laughter.

However, when we finally saunter over to the platform, something else happens. A huge gust of wind tears at the fistful of papers in the architect's hand. There is a ripping noise and Pratt is so startled, he drops the box. Seizing its opportunity, the wind claims them all. Glossy colour brochures and posters jerk past us in waves and zigzags, like a paper storm enveloping us all, until another powerful gust sweeps them out to sea.

Every last one of them bar the torn bundle of shreds left in *I-am-a-prat*'s hand.

Every last one? No, not quite. One blows across and catches under my shoe. I smooth out the crumpled paper as I push it into my jacket pocket.

I think I may keep it. A souvenir of the day Dr Pratt made himself ridiculous.

Later that afternoon I walk through the creaky metal door into our hut and see him sitting at our kitchen table. *Oh wonderful! What's he doing here?* I nearly say aloud, but instead I throw my bag into the corner and smile. 'Hey, Dr Pratt.' My parents should be proud of me and my impeccable social skills. Even more so as I don't strangle him when he completely ignores me. Sometimes I'm surprised at my self-control.

Since there's no room for me to sit anywhere near the table anyway, I grab a glass of juice and a biscuit and head for my room. My door slams shut and the hushed voices resume their normal volume, as if any danger of being overheard had gone.

Of course, I can hear every word. I can even hear

when Pratt begins chewing another biscuit. Gross.

Reaching over for my headphones, I'm about to block it all out when something about the way Dad is speaking catches my attention.

'Ian, I'm not sure that we can just carry on as if nothing's happened here. Would it make such a difference if we got someone to check it out for a couple of days? Whatever it is, it's a protected…'

'No. No, Will. I hear what you're saying, I really do, but we're already behind. I don't think there's any value in looking too closely at whatever they are. It could take months, especially if anyone decides it's worth looking more closely.'

Mum's soft voice mingles with the clinking of the teapot on cups. 'More cake? I was just wondering—who would be in charge of this sort of thing anyway?'

'We do NOT need to take this thing further, and that's the final word on the matter. Now, let's talk about the foundations instead. So, these reinforcement cages…'

Dad hesitates but decides to give in for the moment. 'If we push on, they should be in by next weekend. Ready to pour the concrete the week after, if…'

'Yes, if the weather holds. It's likely to be all right—I checked the long-term forecast.'

'Good,' says Dad, sounding almost aggressive.

There is a long pause.

'I'd better be going…' squeaks the architect and I hear

scraping across the floor and mumbled apologies as the three adults fold chairs and bump into each other in the process. The door creaks once again and I peek out of the window to watch *I-am-a-prat* stride past Anna and Catriona to his individual little pod, reserved just for him. I try to imagine the kind of house he would live in in London. *No. Stop. Any time spent thinking about that man is wasted. He's almost as annoying as…*

Mum and Dad still stand crouched over the cooker and whispering when I burst in.

'Have you… seen Struan at all? Since school, I mean.'

CHAPTER SEVEN

SEARCH

At least this time they are not just ignoring me. Mum has woken Izzy from her afternoon nap and is carrying her on her hip whilst going door to door along every hut. Dad is scouring the bay, especially down by the rocks. I run back to school which takes me all of thirty seconds. Mr Johnston isn't in. I didn't expect him to have left already, but it figures—school finished about an hour ago. I could kick myself! How could I not notice that Struan wasn't behind me? How could I just listen to Pratt rattling on and not realise that the noisiest person in our family wasn't there? The noisiest person on this whole god-forsaken island—probably even the world! I'm sure it's to do with being the eldest, but I feel it's my fault. Who am I kidding? It *is* my fault. What if something's happened to him? Only when I'm imagining my brother's lifeless little body grinding against rock in the sea do I notice that I'm still in the classroom. The last few embers smoulder in the stove.

Through the gathering rain, I see Mum and Dad pointing at the school hut.

They're waiting for me.

Paralysed by worry, I force myself back out in the open and shake my head. That's all it takes. Like a spring released, Dad runs to the storehouse and begins ringing a large bell by the door. I'd never even realised it was there, but in seconds, he is surrounded by a sea of people, worry etched on their faces.

'We've got a bit of an emergency, I'm afraid. Struan's gone missing. We've checked the obvious places, but no luck so far. I wonder if any of you could help us search?'

There is an immediate murmur and a handful of people sprint back to their huts to turn off cookers and fetch jackets.

Dad begins again. 'Are any other kids gone?'

People shake their heads. They obviously don't want to look him in the eye.

'OK, let's...' and then his voice finally falters and he presses his lips really tightly together, the way I've only ever seen once, at Grandad's funeral. Mum looks like a ghost. Izzy is being bundled to Petra's hut, so Mum can join the search. *It's a dream, just a dream, just a hideous, awful dream...*

'All right, let's swarm out and make the most of the light.' Mr Johnson has appeared and taken charge. 'If the two of you head towards the Ben...'—he nods to Jeff and Hughie, the apprentices who share the small hut by the pier. He sends two other teams along the seashore in opposite directions. Dad and Harvey are walking along the cliff tops and the rest of us are given the pier, the huts, the flat moorland and the wood. Petra offers to look after all the children in her hut. Mum begins to sway slightly so that Muriel has to catch her and she ends up staying with Petra, too. All this is arranged in less than two minutes, and we're off. *Where would he go?* None of his little friends have any idea at all. Zac and I head for the wood, yelling at the top of our voices, but the wind simply carries the sound away. Heavy, cold rain begins to fly at me with savage force; I'm not even wearing a jacket.

'Here!' yells Zac over the wind and throws me his. Can he read minds? I shake my head and try to give it back but he yells something at me again.

'What?'

'My fleece is waterproof. It's OK. STRUAN!'

'STRUAN!' I join in, and like an eerie choir, fragments of voices all around Skelsay join us, faint in the distance. *What if, somewhere, Struan is calling, too? Calling for help… his words drowned by the wind?*

I yell again with all my might. Almost an hour passes while Zac looks every tree up and down, as if my brother could be sitting above, laughing at us all. But he wouldn't do that! Even Struan, surely, wouldn't do that!

41

Then a whistle pierces through the turbulent air. I hear shouting too, but it's too faint to make out. Zac's face tells me he's not sure what it means either. We both strain to listen. More voices join, nearer this time.

'Found! Pass it on!'

We turn to each other and smile. Guilty boulders the size of Skelsay itself roll from my burdened conscience and I shout, as loudly as I can: 'FOUND! Pass it on!'

You'd think we'd be trudging back slowly after a search like this, but I sprint all the way, narrowly beating Zac to the square. The rain is easing off a bit now, and there are voices nearby, behind the barrier to the building site.

'I thought we weren't allowed in there,' says Zac and I shrug. I see Mum with Izzy on her hip, inside the workers' enclosure.

'I'm going over.'

'Em, wait,' he begins but I run ahead and my friend has no choice but to follow me.

By now there must be ten of us, standing around the dug-out foundation pit waiting for its reinforcement cage. There is a tarpaulin over it, which Erica is holding up high enough for me to see my brother crouching beneath. Dad is down in the pit beside him, his face alive with rage.

An hour later I've decided to go to bed early. Mum and Dad's lecture relay is still going on and Struan's cheeks are crusty with dried up tears.

'I just saw you all bent over that bit during school. I thought you might have found something interesting,' Struan hiccups in defence, but Dad's having none of it.

'You are not allowed to go past that barrier. Ever. You knew that, Struan!'

'I thought a couple of minutes wouldn't matter, just after school. And when I saw the cave, I tried to dig down a bit more for closer look, but they weren't moving...'

'Struan, you were gone for over two hours! And we were shouting for you!'

'Well, I didn't hear you, honestly. The rain was coming down and that plastic sheet thing was right over my head. And I was busy digging. And the rain made me feel a bit sleepy and so...' Struan checks himself, as if something new has just popped into his head. 'Dad? What are you going to do? Are we going to dig them out?'

'I don't know yet,' grumbles my father. 'Get to bed now, and don't you dare argue. Now, Struan!'

Quiet obedience is not what my brother is famous for, but he mutely brushes his teeth and slinks into his room. I know the nightly sounds: the latch of Snarl's cage clicks—my brother crumbles some food into the bowl but closes the cage again immediately, without letting the hamster run free like he does any other night. The mattress creaks and the light switch snaps off straightaway. I hear it all, including the muffled hiccups that go on and on.

I lie still, facing the ceiling and wondering. My parents whisper to each other in low, intense voices. *Will I risk it? Not yet.*

At 10.30pm it is finally inky black outside and curiosity gets the better of me. Stealthily, I tiptoe across the room, turn the handle and creep into the narrow hall.

Through the crack in the door I can make out Dad at the table, taking notes. Mum is in the bathroom. I wait until I hear the flushing sound before I turn Struan's handle and dive into the darkness.

'Shhhhhhh, Struan!'

There is a slight creak as Mum sinks into bed, but the hamster wheel is turning like it does every night, masking my steps. I hold my breath and wriggle to the space where Struan's head may be. I wish I could see better.

'Struan?'

I hear the shuffle as he moves closer and touches my face.

'All right?' I whisper. No answer, but he wriggles even closer to me and I ruffle his hair in silence. Through the wall, I hear Dad turn on the radio. We both exhale with relief.

'So, wee man. Tell me then. What is it that they've found?'

CHAPTER EIGHT

INTEGRITY

Of course, I can't pretend I don't know about the hibernating bats and the cave our guys have accidentally dug into, especially not now, so I ask Dad the next day. To my surprise, he is in an ebullient mood. Dad hates uncertainty. I know that look—he's made up his mind about something.

'Sure, you can see them. In fact, you all will soon. There is a guy from Scottish Natural Heritage coming tomorrow, with some Bat Trust people, too. Exciting isn't it?'

I am so gobsmacked that I turn right round and wander off towards school. Struan is already there, telling his adoring audience the details, all eyes in the room fixed on him in rapt attention. He can talk without even breathing, I swear it's true.

'...and that's why I thought I'd sneak under the tarpaulin and check it out. Man, you've never seen anything this cool before; there is a proper cave below the site. No, really, there is! It was dark and there was dirt all over it and so I used my hands to dig the hole a bit wider and then I saw them hanging there upside down, like mice with wings, although it was a bit dark and I couldn't quite see properly. But they had their wings folded over like this...' He attempts to demonstrate with his arms.

I clear my throat. He's got them all wrapped round his little finger; even Mr Johnston is not doing anything to shut him up.

'What's your Dad's plan then?' asks Zac beside me.

'Not sure, but he's got some people coming to look at it.'

Both of us look up, startled at the sound of the approaching chopper. I completely forgot that Pratt was leaving again. We all rush to the window and Mr Johnston doesn't stop us. Pratt and Dad are having their usual farewell chat, only they're shouting, loudly enough for us to hear through the plexi-glass.

'Look Ian, I just won't! Not only is it illegal; it's an integrity issue. We'll make up the time.'

I-am-a-prat says something rude about integrity and yells 'You'd better!' before the helicopter drowns him out. Mud flies, the machine lands and in another roar of the engine, he is gone. Dad's already walking back to the hut, kicking a stone out of the way, hard.

That evening, when I get back from playing hide-and-seek with the little ones, Mum is sitting at the tiny table sketching gulls. Izzy has begun to crawl and is zooming round and round and round Mum's feet—probably because there isn't anywhere else to go.

'Hmmnnnn!' My mother half-mumbles, half sings. She's in the zone. Normally, the surface would be covered in tins and vegetable peelings, but all is pristine and clear.

I consider this. In Glasgow, coming back to a kitchen like this at 5.30pm meant going out for dinner. *I wonder where the nearest Pizza Place is.*

The crunching steps outside signal Dad's arrival. *Are the bat experts with him? Doesn't sound like it.*

'Right, Karen, you ready? Oh, good, Em, you're back! Listen, you'll need an extra jumper, and be quick. Struan is already down there.'

Down where?

Before I can ask, Mum snaps into action, her hands moving like lightning bolts and electrifying the cabin in an instant.

'Oh, help, is that the time? Sorry Will; got a bit side-tracked! Em, why haven't you got your jacket on yet? And grab that jumper Dad told you to get, or are you deaf today? Oh, and on your way out, take the packets of sausages over there; they should be defrosted by now. To the beach, to the beach. Quick, go, go, go!'

My wee sister whines as Mum attacks her with her little coat, wrapping her in another layer of a fluffy snowsuit and finishing off the package with a stripy knitted hat.

'MOVE, Em; everyone's waiting!' Dad is practically out of the door again.

Finally, I snap into action. *Jumper: check. Jacket: check.* They didn't tell me to bring gloves, but *gloves: check*, anyway.

Mum slams the cabin door behind us and we bundle down the verge onto the beach.

Oh, for goodness' sake!

I spin round. Thirty seconds later, I bolt down the hill again.

Sausages: check.

CHAPTER NINE

DELAY

After about five attempts, and I don't know how many matches, the bonfire finally takes. Some off-cuts of wood from the site soon smoulder in the breeze and golden flames funnel upwards beside the sea through the driftwood. Above us, the clouds, too, glow orange, pink and purple as the fireball of the sun sinks towards the horizon out west. Nice idea, the beach party thing. Dad's brain-wave, apparently. Struan says it's in honour of the Scottish Natural Heritage people, but really, it's pretty obvious that Dad's just having a bash, now that Pratt's finally gone.

All of the kids buzz out like bees and return with armfuls of driftwood and whatever else they think may burn.

'Hey! Em! Over here! Do you think you could…?'

Gasping with effort, Zac comes into view, dragging some kind of gigantic tree trunk—and I'm on my feet. It takes both of us five minutes to haul, push and roll the monstrosity to the bonfire, mainly because we keep collapsing in fits of giggles.

Dad narrows his eyes and raises his eyebrows. 'Are you serious? That'll never burn!'

'I know. But check it out, right?' And to demonstrate, Zac flops down onto the trunk, groaning in fake comfort and stretching his hands towards the warming flames.

'Ah, a seat; I get it! Very good, young man! You'll go far, mark my words.' Dad and two of the visitors sit down beside him, shuffling along to make room for me. The apprentices have started a game of football with the boys and Petra brings out a guitar as sparks rise, again and again, into the darkening sky.

'Cool! Can I have a go?' Zac's fired the question before Petra has even played a note herself, but at least he has the decency to look a bit ashamed. 'Sorry,' he mumbles at once.

'You play, do you? Ah. I see. Yours was in that container, right?' Petra hands him the instrument, and for the first and only time, I see a flutter of pain in Zac's nod. Not for his Mum or his Dad, but for himself. And soon I understand.

He's brilliant at it, that's why. The gentle surf of the sea keeps the beat and we jig as his fingers dance across the frets.

'Listen, Zac, you keep hold of that guitar for the time being, OK? I hardly get a chance to play it anyway. I'm sure you'll get more use out of it. Hungry, anyone?' Petra rises and brings out a sealed container.

'What on earth is *that*?'

OK, maybe I shouldn't have said that aloud. 'Sorry, it's just…'

The slimy bubbling mass oozes over the rim in stringy drops. *I'd rather starve than eat that!*

'Pass me the sticks. I've done this before.' Petra reaches for a pile of sticks at my feet and wraps the end of it in foil. She reaches into the foul container and pulls out a messy handful, wrapping it around the covered stick in a thin layer.

'Stick bread!' she announces. 'Have you never seen this? We do it all the time in Germany.' She holds her rod over the fire and rotates it slowly.

It takes me and Zac much longer to copy her, but the mixture of fresh bread and salty sea will be my favourite smell until the day I die.

'Aaaaah, good. Food! Let's get the sausages on. Come on, lads,' shouts Harvey. We dunk our charred bread in butter and sip hot chocolate from the flask, and life is about as good as I can imagine, especially when Harvey reveals a set of bagpipes from his holdall. He plays tune after tune, with Struan at his feet.

'That's the loudest thing I've ever heard,' my brother says in awe. 'Can you teach me?'

'Sure—I've got a couple of chanters with me in case

someone fancied it. I'll pop round tomorrow if you like.'

Struan's eyes shine, and our singing carries on late into the night. And when we're all sung out, sitting quietly by the dying embers, warm inside and out, a solitary otter makes an appearance out in the bay, leaving v-shaped ripples in its wake.

Our adventure on an island...

This is certainly more like it.

After two weeks, the team from Scottish Natural Heritage have made the cave safe, gently moving the bats into a different chamber of the cave and sealing the hole off. By the beginning of April, Dad is getting tense, and not just because Struan has become obsessed with chanter-playing. The workers need to get on with it, and fast. The last few weeks have been fairly dry, which was good for the conservation work, but now the serious business begins.

Building the Skelsay Skies resort.

One afternoon after school I take nine messages for Dad on his satellite phone. Of course, all of them are from *I-am-a-prat*'s secretary, Lorena. Her posh accent makes everything she says sound terribly urgent. Dad chuckles and rolls his eyes when I tell him, doing my best to imitate her voice.

'The metal cages are in,' he announces. 'Now we're ready to pour foundations.'

'Really?' says Mum from behind her easel. I can tell she's not really that interested.

Mum's paintings are becoming a bit of an issue. The storehouse can be damp and she wants to play safe and keep them in here. There are at least fifteen canvases under my bed, and Struan has the smaller ones in his wardrobe.

'Yes, REALLY! All we need now is a decent run of good, dry weather. And no frost, that's all I ask.'

'What's the forecast?' I ask and Dad turns as if he sees me for the first time that night.

'Supposed to be all right, so they say. Fingers crossed. Thanks for asking.'

I wake up to find the world dusted in frost. In fact, I think it is Dad's painful yelp that wakes me. That gas heater can't be working very well—I can see my own breath. I'm still trying to persuade myself to creep out from under my duvet when I hear Dad thundering out of the cabin—without stopping for breakfast—or even a cup of tea. He slams the door. The moss crunches under his feet as he stomps away.

Breakfast would have been a quiet affair if it hadn't been for Struan yapping on about sledging and igloos and ice fortresses. Izzy, who has discovered the art of saying actual words, tries to repeat everything he says. They have even given Snarl an extra wad of cotton wool for warmer bedding—sort of like a pet version of an extra duvet. 'I wish I was a hamster,' I grumble through chattering teeth.

My brother doesn't seem to have heard me; he is still in full flow. 'And what about snowboarding? I bet I'd be really good at it. Maybe I could try.'

'Oh, grow up, Struan! It's a bit frosty, but there won't be proper snow—not now. It's April!'

Towering clouds gather behind the curtains.

Trudging to school, I see Dad, Harvey and a few others, standing in a crowd around the concrete mixer. All are wrapped tightly in their identical high-vis jackets, hats pulled down far over the ears. I can tell my father by the hunched shoulders. The wind is fierce and the first stray snowflakes dance around us in triumph. I run the last few steps to the school cabin.

Most of us arrive slightly late. Mr Johnston is crouching in front of the stove, stacking kindling.

'I'm not taking my coat off! It's baltic in here!'

'Me neither. Can't you put the heating on Mr Johnston?'

'What do you think I'm doing, Anna?' Mr Johnston replies, almost cheerfully. Strange man!

I try to do my equations wearing my gloves.

'Look!' Struan points suddenly, and as one, we rush to the big window. The air is solid white, it seems—I have never, ever seen snowfall this dense before. All the younger ones' voices skip over one another:

'Magic,' shouts Mikey.

'Can we go home, Mr Johnston? I can't see my cabin anymore,' Catriona begs.

'Hey—let's build a snow fortress!'

Struan's last comment is met with universal applause from his disciples who reach for their jackets. Mr Johnston clears his throat loudly.

'Erm… at break time, I mean,' adds Struan.

Zac is staring at the sea—or the place where the sea would be if we could see it. He's not said a word since he got here. 'Zac? What is it?' I whisper.

'For one thing it's weird. Just weird. But on top of that, the supply boat is due today.'

It takes me a while to work out what he is saying, but eventually, the meaning of it all trickles through. Of course. Food. And mail. And also…

'Is some more of your gear coming today? New clothes and stuff?'

'Yep. And a million other things too—course books for Mum's Open University, for example. I hope they make it through. I don't think Mum could take it if they didn't.'

Zac is quite sweet like that, I think, so protective of Muriel. If that was me, I'd think only about myself and that would be it. I resolve to be a much better daughter.

'Right, everyone, we *were* going to plant some seeds

today and research the life cycle of various plants, but maybe that will have to wait. So, let's see what the Met Office have to say about this cold spell, shall we? This kind of freak weather in spring should make an interesting topic to investigate. Now, cast your minds back to February when we covered weather in geography. And in your case, Em and Zac, you should remember all about cold fronts? Lows? Cloud formation? I'll be calling on you to explain the process to the younger ones.'

Vague diagrams of rising air assemble in my mind while I wait for the image to load.

The screen flickers and for a moment I think it isn't going to work. Then a map of Scotland appears and Mr Johnston zooms in on the West Coast and Skelsay.

'Right, Zac. I want you to explain to the rest of the class why...'

He stops, speechless.

Actually, we're *all* speechless. The symbol over our island is a sun. Not a cloud in sight—there's high pressure over the whole of Scotland. On Skelsay it's supposed to be 14 degrees Celsius and sunny.

We all jump when the gale rattles the door open and a flurry of snow blows into the room.

CHAPTER TEN

JINXED

Zac and I spend all morning trying to figure it out. When I nip home at lunchtime, Dad is busy finding fault with *everything*, from his shaver to the bread bin, from the leaky tap (which doesn't bother him normally) to Struan's wellies which he tripped over. I head back to school almost immediately before he has a proper meltdown.

Mr Johnston has left the light on over break as it's so dark with all the cloud cover. Within minutes, Zac arrives too and we set to work again, checking webcams on nearby islands. Glasgow is basking in glorious sunshine, I note grumpily. Skye is quite sunny, so are Harris and Lewis. The Uists are positively tropical. *What's happening?*

In a strange way, I'm almost excited. It's the kind of thing that would happen in a book. In a film, even. Not in real life.

But it is happening here.

'It's like we're jinxed on this island,' I quip.

There is a long, very long pause as both of us process this possibility.

The seals. The container. The sea. Those bats choosing a place beneath our very foundations to hibernate. The freezing cold and wet, when all we need is dry.

'I was only joking,' I add, mostly to myself.

'Yeah, yeah. I know, haha,' Zac agrees lamely.

But we're on to something.

I can feel it.

On the way home after school Struan makes snow angels and boasts that his underwear is still wet from sledging at lunchtime. Admittedly, it did look fun, though I'm surprised no-one broke their neck. The apprentices managed to get hold of a tyre tube and allowed Struan and his gang to join in. I've never seen anything on land move so fast. They got a full twenty minutes of it before Mr Johnston started barking at the apprentices about health and safety from one side and Dad stomped over from the other, tearing them to shreds about keeping spare tubes in prime condition for future use. And that was the end of that.

Still, it doesn't appear to have put too much of a dampener on Struan's mood.

'So—what do you reckon, Em? Will this carry on? Hey, do you think they might close the school if it snows enough? I wonder if Mum's gonna let me stay out until it's dark. Gregor says he's allowed and he's only a year older than me...'

Dad is on his mobile when we walk in. By the time I've taken off my shoes and coat, a puddle of melt water has formed around my feet, but any sympathy I expected from my mother doesn't materialise. Instead, her eyes are fixed on Dad who is bouncing around the room like a punctured balloon. I had thought this place was too small to pace, but there you have it.

'I've just said the same to the receptionist. No, it's not good enough. Listen, we've got families here, not just the workforce. Can't you just...'

Dad holds the receiver away from his ear while someone rants at the other end, rolling his eyes at Mum.

'Finished? Right, listen. You say you can't get through. *I* say you're not trying hard enough. Not nearly hard enough! You do realise I'm going to take this right to the top, don't you? You leave me no choice. I'd rather not, but...'

Izzy has started whimpering and Mum's heading to the sink for a beaker of juice. Remembering about being a much better daughter, I lift my sister up from the floor and take her towards my room to give Dad some peace. Mum smiles at me gratefully. I nearly drop Izzy when Dad yells at the top of his voice:

'DON'T you DARE hang up on me!'

There is a pause while I recover my balance.

His voice is no more than a mumble when he speaks again.

'He's hung up. The supply boat is not coming.'

I've never seen my father looking so utterly defeated before.

The place is full of gossip the next morning. People stop to talk wherever they can and every snippet of conversation bristles with frustration.

Any word of the supply boat? Ah. I thought as much.

How much is left in the storehouse? And how long will that last us?

Any sign of better weather? What does the Met Office say?

Who knows? The internet's gone down.

What? How am I supposed to pass my course if I can't get online?

Called a meeting, did he?

Tonight, is it?

What are we going to do? Have you got any spare gas cylinders?

No, me neither. We're already rationing the heating, but they're bloody cold, these cabins.

Can you believe it's nearly May? World's gone mad, eh?

Zac is quieter than normal, but I guess I know why.

'Did your mum take it really bad?' I venture at break.

He takes a bite from an oatcake. 'It won't kill us. We've done without all that stuff for weeks now. Dad says it's probably no bad thing—lets you see how little you really need when it boils down to it. But we are going to have to be careful with the supplies.'

'I guess. They're bound to come soon though. This weather can't last forever.'

We exchange a glance and there it is again, hanging in the stillness—the thing we stumbled on yesterday and won't mention now. *I* think about it. I know *he's* thinking about it.

Jinxed.

Neither of us speak until the bell goes again.

That night, the five of us sit around the tiny table, hunched over bowls of canned vegetables and toast while dreaming of proper dinners.

'Do I have to eat all of the beans?' whines Struan, but my parents just ignore him, their tense foreheads barely masking their fears.

The hamster wheel whirrs gently from my brother's room. Unusually, he doesn't even try to practise the chanter.

He'd probably be murdered if he did.

CHAPTER ELEVEN

TRACKS

There's another meeting, this time in the school, which is the only cabin with a hope of holding all of us. We're packed in like hot dogs in a jar. The last two people are just shuffling in and shaking wet snow from their hoods as Dad begins.

No smile, no introduction. Straight to it.

'Bad weather. OK, it's a setback, but we've no choice but to sit this out. Hopefully it will not be too long—I don't have to tell you that conditions like these are highly unusual for late spring. We could have done without this though; I've got Prime Isles breathing down my neck to make progress. And the architect's due here again in just over a week.'

There are suppressed groans from a couple of corners, but Dad ignores them and soldiers on. 'Dr Pratt will expect to see foundations poured and proper construction underway. And, with even a tiny bit of luck, we can give him that. We'll have to put in a fair bit of overtime when the weather finally improves, but it can be done. Until then, there is nothing we can do but rest and wait.'

He clears his throat before proceeding. 'There is, however, a more serious issue.'

Quiet creeps into every last corner of the room. Even the two toddlers seem to be holding their breath.

'As you know, the supplies come from the mainland on a Tuesday. They were unable to reach us today, and a technical problem prevented them coming last time. They've just been in touch to say they will not attempt to come until next week.'

I expected gasps or groans but, somehow, the heavy hush is worse.

'Their vessels are committed elsewhere later in the week and, according to the idiot on the other end of the phone, we are not an emergency yet.'

I look around. Harvey whispers something to the pale-faced, tight-lipped Muriel whose hair is even frizzier than normal. Zac is staring out of the window. Mum keeps stepping back and forwards, trying to settle Izzy. My sister is getting a bit heavy to carry now.

'And there is a final, potentially quite serious issue which most of you don't know about yet.'

Anxious glances are exchanged around the room. This is probably the longest Struan has ever held his tongue in his life.

'It's not a secret that the storehouse is running low on most of the basics. However, it seems that, on top of everything else, we have a bit of a rodent problem.'

It's as if a shell has fallen. We are dumbstruck as the impact of these words sinks in, but soon there are giggles of relief and even quiet chatter. *What can be so bad? There were mice in Glasgow—we had them in the shed. No big deal! Surely...*

'It appears that the problem is on quite a large scale... We are talking mice, rats, voles and, erm, weasels if Roger here—' (he points at Mr Johnston) '—is right about the droppings. There is no usable flour left, I'm afraid, and that's just an example.'

That shuts up all the chatterers. Including me.

We're going to starve.

Later, we have beans on toast—again. Thankfully, the bread's fine—we keep it in the gigantic freezer chest in the storehouse. Come to think of it, it would probably still freeze outside. I'm wrapped up in two jumpers and a blanket—Dad insisted we switch the gas heater off. 'We need to save energy. No way around it. If it stays cold much longer we'll run into serious problems.'

Porridge for breakfast. It comes dry in big, sturdy tins; safe even from rodents' teeth. The adults spent hours last night, blocking holes and crevices, but the rest of the breakfast cereals were spoilt anyway. Mum and I go in to do a general check.

'Gosh, Em, I really don't know what we'd do without that freezer—we'll need to ration the stuff in there, that's for sure.'

'Honestly, I'm gonna be sick. Mum!' The smell gets me; it's foul.

I can't look at a single surface without gagging. There are droppings everywhere. 'Mum, I'm serious; I'm properly grossed out! I can't stay. Unless you want me to pass out.'

My vision has gone a bit fuzzy, but as far as mothers go, she's pretty rubbish at sympathy. She ignores my last comment and continues briskly. 'All right then. Go round all the cabins and make a list of what everyone needs for the next three days. Exact quantities, please. After that we're just going to have to do the best we can.'

I roll my eyes and stomp off, but to be honest, I'm glad to be out of the storehouse. At least out here the air is fresh.

I start with the apprentices. By the time I've knocked on half the doors, my list is beginning to spill over the page. I leave Zac's hut till last. I'm not proud of it, really, but there is only so much misery I can take.

'Please, please don't let it be Muriel' is my coward's prayer. I knock and the door opens almost immediately.

'Oh, hello Muriel.' I force a smile.

'Morning, Em. Zac's not actually in right now. He's gone for a wee wander towards the woods, but he said he wouldn't go far...' There is a weird, slightly manic cheerfulness to her tone, like someone who is trying a little bit too hard.

I clear my throat. 'Actually, Mum sent me to see you. Could you make a list of the things you will need from the storehouse in the next three days? Mum says the stuff is probably safer in your hut than out there.'

She takes a while. I probably shouldn't, but I count the number of times she blows her nose while she rummages in that kitchen. Nine.

'Nasty cold,' she lies.

Mum is still in the storehouse. The door is wide open for air, but I don't cross the threshold again. Instead, I leave the list on the step and place a rock on it to stop it blowing away. 'Here you go. Done!'

From a distance, I see Zac waving from the edge of the trees and wave back. *Hang on, no. He's not waving. He's beckoning.*

I glance back. Dad's in a meeting, Mum's in the storehouse, Struan's at Tom's, and Izzy's being looked after by Petra...

I think I'll risk it. I'll be back before they even know I'm gone.

Zac stands still, but as soon as I'm within earshot, he shouts. 'Em! Come here! You've got to see this.'

'All right!' I yell back, irritated and wheezing. 'What?'

He points down to the snow at our feet, punctured by melt drops from the trees above us, and pauses dramatically. A few seconds tick by.

'Zac, what are you on about?'

'Oh, Em, for goodness' sake! Will you just look at that!'

Slowly, my eyes grow wide and I feel sick all over again.

'That's... impossible...'

CHAPTER TWELVE

MISSION

Later that night, I lay out everything I need.

Three layers of fleece, two pairs of trackies, a hat and my phone. I check it all again just to be sure and then plug it in. It'll need to be fully charged if I want the torch and the camera to work properly.

Finally, I set the alarm. Volume adjusted low, I place it right beside my pillow. I pull up my blanket and turn off the light, satisfied at last. But sleep doesn't come.

Whenever I close my eyes, I see the scene from the woods again. Tracks in the snow, not of one, two or three, but of *hundreds* of creatures: rats, mice, voles, whatever else. Like an army, all their little trails point in one direction. Towards the building site. The cabins.

Us.

Giant-sized beasts with protruding teeth and sharp claws advance on me, their tails snaking towards my feet like snares. What are these monsters? I hit out, but my fists only find phantoms. Still, the teeth feel real enough when they snap at my sleeves. I run; it's the natural thing to do, but the creatures drop from trees, rise out of roots and shoot up from shingle.

When the phone alarm buzzes, I jerk up, covered in sweat. I imagine Zac doing the same just a stone's throw away in his own cabin. Wonder what kind of night he's had.

Not great either by the looks of it when we meet halfway between our huts fifteen minutes later.

I whisper: 'You look terrible!'

'Says Miss Glam,' he deadpans back.

I feel self-conscious all of a sudden with all my fleecy layers. 'Let's go.'

He shines his phone torch onto the ground. For once, luck is on our side—the wind is blowing in our direction from the forest.

We tiptoe across our settlement, avoiding any crunchy gravel and remnants of ice. The moon hangs like a pale lantern far above, reflecting in small patches of snow.

'Lights off now?' Zac whispers.

'All right.'

We don't talk. Staying upright in the near-complete darkness takes all the concentration we can muster.

The storehouse cabin seems much taller in the dark. Every few steps, we stop to listen.

'You got it?' Zac's voice is barely audible now.

'Yep!' I fumble in my pocket for the key—at least the

fleeces don't rustle.

We both flinch when we hear a sharp noise inside, a snap followed by a whimpering squeak.

'Traps. Don't worry, Zac. I saw Dad carrying an armful to the storehouse in the afternoon.'

'I'm not worried,' my friend hisses back.

'Shh!'

We barely breathe as I insert the key, carefully feeling with my fingers all around the lock. It's as if the ground is moving beneath our feet. I squint to see, but here, away from the moonlight, the blackness swallows everything.

'Ready?' I ask.

'Ready.' Zac nods and begins the count as agreed. 'One... two... THREE!'

I throw the door open and light flashes into the room from Zac's phone torch. It takes me a couple of seconds to work out what I am seeing. Everything in the storehouse is moving. No, every surface in the room is covered by creatures, and *they* are moving. *I'm going to faint. I'm sure of it.*

The air is thick with the stench of unspecified muck. Time has slowed, just to let me sense every stringy tail slide against my ankles. Clammy fur soils my skin with every rodent which writhes and wriggles past me out into the night. Something clambers up my trousers and I scream, shaking my leg in blind panic.

Zac makes a gulping, retching kind of sound, but then he elbows me hard. 'Camera!'

I fumble to find the button. My bobble hat drops to the ground and is carried along by the current of stinking brown bodies around my feet.

'NOW!' Zac shouts, clicking on his phone, but it is barely worth it. The beasts move at lightning speed, disappearing through the open door, up walls, under bottom shelves, into corners, out of sight.

I'm barely aware of anything anymore. All I know is that my legs are carrying me away, away, away. Stumbling and gulping in the cold, fresh air, I nearly pull our cabin door off its hinges.

My father tells me that he has never seen my face so white as when I shake him awake that night.

'Calm it, Em. That's it. Breathe.' Mum is rubbing my back and I am sobbing like a baby. I howl out my terror and cry out my fear, while Dad sits across the bed, furrowing his forehead. He pushes a glass of water at me.

'There you go. Slowly now...' Mum soothes. I am nearly thirteen, but right now I might as well be Izzy's age. I just want to be held. That's pretty much it.

Dad's having none of it. 'Drink up and then we'll talk.'

I need to tell them but I can't.

'Em, listen. You may think you're practically an adult, but you can't sneak out with boys like that. I didn't think you were that interested in boyfriends yet, but I suppose we should have seen the signs...'

Hang on.

What...

It's amazing how outrage can concentrate the mind.

'What the hell are you talking about?' I shout through my tears. 'Do you think if I was going on a midnight date, I'd be wearing this?'

My parents look at each other sheepishly.

Struan pops his head around the door. 'It's three o'clock in the morning,' he corrects.

'Back to bed, Struan. Now!' My mother sounds as tired as I feel, but nowhere near as angry.

'Now, listen to me, Dad. We don't just have a little problem with some mice or rats in the storehouse. There are hundreds of them. Probably thousands. Zac and I decided to check it out because we saw their tracks at the edge of the forest. Like an army, Dad, all heading here. We...'

But my knees wobble beneath me and Mum pushes me down into the soft seat.

'Maybe that's enough for tonight, Will,' Mum suggests. 'Em's just a bit confused and...'

'NO! See for yourself! I have never been less confused in my life!'

Livid, I thrust my phone into Mum's lap.

It takes Dad a while to find the cable that connects

it to the laptop, but eventually, dark images full of shadows inhabit the screen. 'There you are. See?' I say triumphantly, but my parents incline their heads and narrow their eyes.

'Hmmm. Can't really make anything out on these. Can you, Karen?'

Luckily for my father, Mum bundles me off to bed before I get a chance to lunge at him.

CHAPTER THIRTEEN

WAR

'We'll need poison. That'll soon sort them out.'

Dad is on the phone with *I-am-a-prat*.

Mum gestures to Struan and me to be quiet. It's 7.30 in the morning and none of us has slept a wink since I made my dramatic entrance during the night. Izzy is grizzling in the corner. The good news is that it seems to be warming up a little—with the first light we can tell that the patches of snow on the hills around us have shrunk.

As soon as the sun is properly above the horizon, there is a knock at the door. 'Morning, Harvey.' Dad chews down the last of his toast and reaches for his jacket. 'Let's do this.'

Over Harvey's shoulder, I see Zac waiting, shuffling from side to side. His face looks a deadly mixture of grey and green.

'I'm coming too, Dad!' I rush to find my wellies before he has the chance to say no, but he is probably past caring. Outside the storehouse there are four dead rats and a mouse: two caught in traps and the rest squashed. If I wasn't such a wimp, I'd take a proper look, but instead I half-close my eyes to blur the bloody details.

Erica arrives from nowhere with a shovel and begins to scrape what's left of the animals off the ground and we follow Dad into the storehouse. It looks as if a tornado has hit. There are ten traps, all with blood-splattered rat bodies. One is still twitching. Dad runs out, grabs the shovel from Erica's hand and puts it out of its misery. Even though I knew what was coming, I wince.

'Bloody hell! Will, come over here. Can you believe this?' Harvey bends over the freezer, his boots half-covered by a gathering icy puddle.

'Don't tell me they've...'

'Yep. They have. Gnawed right through the cable. And here's the dead rat to prove it.' Harvey holds up the electrocuted beast by the tail where it swings gently.

I've heard enough. Zac and I exchange a grimace and flee outside.

The bonfire of dead rodents and contaminated food burns all morning, its smoke mingling with that of the school stove in a murky swirl across the sky.

At mid-day, Dad comes to the school. All of us sit up. He never comes into this building during school hours. Mr Johnston actually breaks off mid-sentence, which is unheard of.

'I just wanted you all to know that the supply boat will try to get through tomorrow. All new foodstuff will be stored in airtight metal containers.'

We all stare.

'It means that, with a bit of luck, there will be plenty of food again,' Mr Johnston translates, and relaxed smiles break out around the room. The younger ones chatter, but Zac and I look at each other darkly.

I run home after school and throw my bag behind the futon.

'Back in a bit!' I yell and race for the edge of the wood where Zac is already waiting. The animal tracks are still there, only just visible in the melting snow. I stamp on them, and then again, hard. *If only everything could be undone so easily.*

'So,' begins Zac.

'Hmmm,' I answer. Now we are here I can't think of anything to say. Or maybe I don't want to say it out loud.

Zac tries again. 'Em, this is serious. How are we going to get them to believe us?'

I shrug my shoulders. 'Believe us? Anyone can tell that there were rats in the storehouse.'

'I don't mean that, Em.'

'What then?'

There is impatience in his eyes. 'I *mean*, Em: HOW are we going to make them believe we are at war with this wilderness? With this island.'

WAR?

I see the tracks again; hear my own words: *"like an army"*.

War. I feel stupid even *thinking* it. How much more of an idiot am I going to feel *saying* it?

'Zac, what's it going to change anyway? We're going to build this stupid resort, aren't we? And then I'll go back to Glasgow and you'll go back to...'

He raises his hands to his head in frustration. 'Em. Think for a minute—please. Think of how this project has started. And everything that has happened since. What do you think might happen next? What is it going to do to make us leave?'

I fold my arms. 'What do you mean, "*it*"?'

My friend's lips are tight for a moment and he looks away. 'I don't know... here. This island? The wilderness? Nature.'

I can't help it, it just sounds so ridiculous and I snort loudly. *I don't want to believe it. I won't believe it. Believing it will make it possible.*

Zac glares at me and turns to walk away, but his hands shake as he zips up his jacket against the sudden chill.

I feel it too.

At 9pm, I bang on the wall. 'Stop that racket, Struan. I'm begging you—mercy!'

'It's not a racket. It's *music*. I have to practise if I want to get better; Harvey says.'

'Maybe Harvey should have picked someone with a musical cell in their body...'

But a deafening chanter-blast puts an end to my argument. *There is nothing I'd rather do than snap that stupid thing in half and throw it back in my brother's smug face.*

I collapse into my bed, but sleep is fitful and light—the air rifle shots of the guards around the storehouse ring out through the night, and Snarl's hamster wheel has developed an irritating scraping sound. Admittedly, thoughts of war don't help either.

It's hard to feel the same anxiety the next morning when the dark wall of cloud is pushed away by a brilliant blue sky. For the first time in over a week, I feel the warmth of the sun on my face.

By lunchtime, Mr Johnston has all but given up expecting any serious effort from us, and when the supply boat finally comes into view around the headland he doesn't even protest when we all run off towards the pier. It seems that all the adults are gathering, too, as huge gas cylinders are wheeled down the narrow ramp, followed by boxes and boxes of supplies. Dad collects a foil-wrapped parcel labelled "rat-poison" in person, but his visage darkens when Ian Pratt appears on deck.

'Surprise! Hello, team!' The architect waves. 'I thought I'd tag on while the helicopter is out of action. Wouldn't want you to get lazy while you're waiting for the good weather.' He grins as if he'd cracked some sort of hilarious joke.

Dad turns on his heel and stamps down towards the site. 'Come on, everyone. We have a bit of clearing up to do. And you kids, get back to school, now.'

A new kind of frost is spreading, make no mistake.

I almost feel sorry for Pratt, abandoned and left to drag his sorry bag of designer clothes down the gangway on his own.

Almost.

CHAPTER FOURTEEN

TIP-OFF

My father stretches back and inhales the warm air. After seven days of solid sunshine, we're getting on top of the rodent problem and, as of this afternoon, the building project is officially back on track. 'That should do it, everyone; that should do it.'

Mr Johnston has brought us all out from the school cabin to watch as the last foundation is poured and begins to set. Normally they'd keep going till six, but Dad's voice is bright. 'Finish here and have a pint. Job well done, thank you all.' A crate of beer appears from somewhere and Mr Johnston is the first to offer Erica a bottle.

I reckon we're dismissed then.

Pratt stands at the side and coughs, ready to make his own speech, but everyone's opening and clinking bottles, chatting and chuckling in the glow of the sun.

And something snaps. The architect throws both his arms up into the air, stamps over to my father and jabs him in the shoulder from behind. 'Will, a word please,' he demands.

Dad steps away from the group with a sigh of resignation. 'Yes, Ian? What can I do for you now?'

'You can't carry on like this, you know. Letting them slack off like that. Don't you see what's at stake here? You need to speed up the process, get ahead. The Prime Isles executives are going to be here in a matter of weeks.'

'We'll be ready, all right? I'm grateful for your concern, but we'll be fine here, Ian. Really.'

Dad sounds anything but grateful, or, come to think of it, fine.

Pratt's voice drips with fake encouragement. 'I'm sure you're doing your best, Will. But if your work is not up to scratch, I have no choice but to make your life difficult. Not that I intend to—nothing could be further from my plans. I just mean that...'

But we never hear what Pratt really means as Dad stomps away to our cabin and slams the door so hard that everyone looks up from their beers.

'Diplomatic!' admires Struan. Someone snorts.

When Pratt's posh pick-up helicopter soars into the clear skies the next morning, Dad actually whistles.

Spring is well and truly here now, and with it, a new school project. Mr Johnston has been exploiting our rodent trouble and the freak weather. We built a weather station halfway up the Ben and the food shortages inspired him to do a quick war project on rationing. All of our maths has been to do with kilos of flour and packets of lentils. *Riveting.*

'Well, I reckon it's time we explored this island's wildlife in more detail,' says Mr Johnston, rubbing his hands together. 'First, we'll make a nature notebook for each of you, and then we'll get going!'

We stare in disbelief. *What does he mean? Watch the grass grow? Does Struan count as wildlife, I wonder?*

Our resident wildlife buff is the only one with a smile on his face: while the rest of us groan and complain under our breaths, Zac has already begun to outline wings, branches, spiders' webs, burrows and nests on the plain notebook Mr Johnston has handed him. *How can he think we're under attack one day and then be excited about the great outdoors the next? I don't get it.*

Mr Johnston speaks eagerly. 'Your homework for tomorrow is to research Skelsay wildlife as best as you can. What are the iconic species? Where are we likely to find them? How can we best protect them? Ask your parents, look it up, google and take notes. Anything will do. Just so long as you come with something. Tomorrow morning we'll confer before we plan the next stage, all right?'

Mr Johnston's eyes blaze and, for a second, it's hard not to feel a tiny, microscopic bit interested. Then I remember that this project will involve lots of standing around in windy places, waiting for stuff to happen while nothing happens at all, and I sigh again.

In the afternoon, the younger ones read while Zac and I learn to do bar graphs and pie charts on the computer, ready to present whatever we find. I can tell: behind his intensely focused face, an avalanche of excitement is waiting to roll, and when the home bell finally goes, I find out why. He points to the edge of the forest.

'All right! Hey, Struan. Tell Mum I'll be back in a few minutes, OK?'

A brief cloud of dust and he's gone. Struan loves home time. *Has he even heard me?*

Zac is tapping his foot by the trees and launches straight into it as soon as I catch up. 'Don't you see? This project is exactly what we need! We're going to find out for certain if there's any truth in… our theory. When we're out and about, we'll *know* if the wilderness is against us, won't we? We can keep a close eye on things, not just be locked up inside some cabin all day. Right?'

'Hang on. *Your* theory, for a start. And I'm not so sure…'

It's a lot harder to believe that the wilderness is out to get us when the wind is still and the sun is shining. The foundations are in, Pratt is gone, Dad is happy. All is as it should be.

'Although…' Zac's eyes dart left and right, up and

down.

'What? For goodness' sake, Zac. Just say it!'

'Well… It could be dangerous, couldn't it? Like wandering into enemy territory in a war or something.'

It's a good few seconds before I realise he's actually being serious. A chill spreads up my back, but all I feel is cold fury.

'You're bonkers,' I whisper, but once I have started, the words pour out of me and I point. 'Face it! You are completely mad, Zac. You read all these nature books and you look at bugs for fun, for crying out loud! What kind of person does that?'

He is probably taken aback by my outburst, and to be honest, so am I, but I still can't stop. 'Of course we're not at war; it's ridiculous, that's what. Spooky, and maybe a little bit cool as a story, but crazy. Grow up, Zac!'

He looks me in the eye, takes a deep breath, zips up his jacket to the very top, turns…

And marches away.

I don't really mind having homework like this. Dad always hogs the computer at night, but as it's for homework, he has no choice but to let me on first, even if I have to look up boring wildlife. At least he has something else to occupy him: Izzy has started talking, which basically means both my parents kneel in front of her and wait for her to speak whenever they've got nothing better to do.

I type *"Skelsay"* into the search engine. Before I've even had the chance to type "wildlife", the drop-down menu offers me *"Skelsay illegal wildlife cull"* as the first option. It's from the Scotland news website. And it's dated today.

Today?

I lean towards the screen.

TODAY?

Unlawful Wildlife Cull on Hebridean Island Revealed

It has been discovered that a building project on the small Hebridean island of Skelsay is endangering protected native wildlife.

No stranger to controversy, Prime Isles Development Ltd bought the uninhabited island ten years ago and has been involved in prolonged legal battles with conservation groups.

Last October, the company obtained planning permission for a hotel and leisure complex with associated facilities and began construction earlier this year.

Guidelines to safeguard the survival of endangered species were agreed to by Prime Isles Development Ltd. This week, however, an anonymous tip-off, reportedly from a project insider, has provided evidence of unlawful killings of species as rare as the black water vole.

Small islands like Skelsay are regarded as crucial havens for the animals which have been all but eradicated on the Scottish mainland by the influx of the American Mink.

A spokesman for the Scottish Wildlife Trust said today: 'This incident obviously needs to be investigated closely, and we will work with the Scottish Government to do just that.'

Prime Isles Development Ltd were unavailable for comment.

'Let me see that,' snaps Dad, who must have been looking over my shoulder.

'Move,' he growls a second later and practically shoves me off the seat. His phone begins to ring. I stretch to pick it up and hand it to him.

'Switch it off!'

I hesitate.

'OFF, I said, Em!'

I wrestle with it for a second before it finally stops beeping. As I flee to my room, I nearly bump into Mum.

'What have you two fallen out over now?' she hisses, as if everything was my fault.

But I barely hear her over the blizzard of questions howling in my head.

Voles? Insider? Tip-off?

What does it all mean?

CHAPTER FIFTEEN

SUMMONS

Dad is in London. 'It's a summons,' Mum says with the kind of grim expression that makes me wish I knew exactly what that word meant. Mental note—google it. This much I've worked out, though—he *had* to go and he didn't get a choice. And he was riled. He always cuts himself shaving when he's riled and there were two plasters on his chin. Some posh helicopter picked him up at lunchtime, but that's about all I know.

To make matters worse, Mr Johnston isn't exactly Mr Understanding this morning when I have no homework to show him. I decide to use the oldest trick in the book: blame your little brother.

'Come on, Mr Johnston, Struan hasn't done that homework either. He didn't even go near the computer last night. There was a lot going on in our house.'

'Oh really? What's this then?' smarts Struan and waves a dog-eared leaflet titled "Hebridean Wildlife" in the air. 'Found it in Mum's folder thing, so I didn't need to use the computer at all.'

There is nothing quite so humiliating as looking at your eight-year-old brother and thinking *wish I'd thought of that!*

I am mightily sorry for myself.

'Zac.'

My whisper is barely audible, but Zac is sitting right beside me, drawing a bar graph of eagle sightings on the various islands of the Hebrides.

'Zac,' I say, slightly louder. His gaze is fixed on the figures on a printout from the RSPB website. He punches some numbers into the calculator and leans over his sheet again.

What's going on?

'Look, I'm sorry I shouted at you. But Zac, I really need to tell you something. For goodness' sake, ZAC!'

I didn't mean to raise my voice like that. Turns out I get to tell Zac nothing, for two reasons.

Number one: Mr Johnston has given me lunchtime detention for talking out of turn. And number two: Zac is refusing to talk to *me*.

Of course, the sun is out and Struan's posse clamber down to the beach. I have to stay inside, tidying the classroom, sharpening all the pencils and putting up with whatever other pointless, pathetic job Mr Johnston can find for me to do.

I actually jump when he sits down on the desk

opposite me, and practically choke on my half-eaten sandwich when he speaks, gently probing.

'All right. Come on, Em. Tell me. What's the real reason you didn't do your homework?'

His bushy eyebrows look like giant hairy caterpillars balancing on his eyes. When he's trying to look all serious, they wriggle. Any other day, I might have laughed out loud. However, today I'm much too angry with him and sorry for myself to respond.

'Goodness, Em, I've never seen you in such a strop.' His voice changes, suddenly warm with pity: 'It is hard growing up. I vaguely remember some of it. Boy-girl trouble?'

That does it!

'Why does everyone think there is something going on with me and Zac? Can't two people just be friends around here? What is it with this stupid island!'

I try to stop myself, I really do, but anyway, out it pours—how Dad had to go away, a proper summons (even though I *still* don't know what exactly that means), how I found the tip-off article online, the secret informer, the fact that Dad's bosses are really angry because the whole thing will take even longer to finish and time is money and that I think Zac is bonkers for thinking we are at war and that now he won't talk to me anymore...

At some point I run both out of breath and out of anger and stop. Mr Johnston is dangling his legs and staring thoughtfully out of the window.

The silence stretches. At long last, Mr Johnston gets up, extends his gangly arms towards the ceiling and smiles.

'Well, I'm glad you've got all that off your chest. Maybe I'll get some work out of you this afternoon, eh?'

Before I can even process any of that, he rings the big bell and the door flies open. Struan.

'I've just been home to tell Mum. She says you're in huge trouble!'

And with this, my darling brother collapses into his seat. Beaming.

Back home, I go straight to my room and bang the door so hard I'm sure it's going to bounce right off the hinges. *See if I care.* I've obviously woken Snarl because I can hear the squeaking of the hamster wheel from Struan's room through the tinny wall.

All this, of course, is designed to avoid a Mum-lecture, but now I get two lectures for the price of one: one for detention at school and another for slamming the door. When I snap my answer, I get a third thrown in for free.

'And while we're at it, Em, I'm pretty disappointed by your attitude. You'd think that a girl your age could see beyond herself a little bit. This whole thing has turned into a bit of a nightmare for your father, and you haven't even had the decency to ask, or show the slightest bit of...'

Her eyes well up, she makes a weird noise in her throat tears spill out over her cheeks. In the living room, Izzy is wailing some words that sound like "stop back", which (in my experience) always means: "Stop it, Struan! Give it back!"

I sigh.

'I'll sort them out, Mum. Have a cup of tea or something.' I hug her from behind and whisper "sorry" before disappearing to round up my siblings.

We're half-way through dinner when Harvey knocks on the door. 'Just doing the rounds, Karen. Get-together in half an hour, by the pier. Any word yet?'

'He'll be back the day after tomorrow, he reckons. He texted just now. We'll have to go ahead and tell them without him. The sooner they know the better. You OK doing this?'

Harvey just nods. 'See you there then. Oh, Karen. If you do speak to him, tell him we'll get to the bottom of this, even if it's the last thing we do.'

There is probably nothing in the world I hate as much as adults not telling me what's going on, especially when it's clearly as much *my* business as it is theirs.

'Finish up, kids,' she mutters distractedly. 'Meeting down by the pier and we're all going.'

Izzy nearly chokes as Struan attempts to shove the remaining half-bowl of spag bol into her mouth but

Mum doesn't even notice. I strap the wee one into her buggy—she is getting too big for it now and puts up a mighty fight—but it'll keep her from wandering off now that she's discovered walking properly. I decide not to bother cleaning the pasta and sauce out of her hair. *If Mum doesn't care, why should I?*

Harvey is waiting by the platform Dad made for *I-am-a-prat* all those weeks ago.

I feel a pang of... I don't know what. *He should be here. My father should be addressing us all at a time like this, not Harvey.*

'I'll make a start, erm, folks, even if we're still waiting for... er... people to arrive.' Harvey is not a natural speaker like Dad, but everyone listens, even the apprentices.

'By now, most of you will have seen the headlines about the illegal wildlife cull, and it'll put our project... on hold once more. Will is in London at the Prime Isles head office. After that, he's meeting with investors in Glasgow and Inverness to explain what went on here, and he'll not be back for a couple of days. He is trying to minimise the damage, you see. Thing is, we've had some, erm, media interest in this area before.'

Struan and I exchange a glance. *The cuttings in Dad's folder.*

Harvey hasn't noticed. His eyes are intense, but his voice is hoarse. 'Right now, the most important thing is figuring out...'

There is a dramatic pause as he loses his nerve slightly. Zac grimaces at his dad.

Harvey clears his throat. '...which one of us is the secret informer.'

Silence.

'Someone must have leaked this to the press. An insider. One of us.' Harvey folds his arms.

I don't know where to look.

No-one knows where to look.

In the middle of all this not-looking-at-anyone, my brain is working furiously. *Who on the island is a total wildlife fan?*

Mr Johnston. And Zac.

Who would be able to tell a water vole from a rat? Mr Johnston. And Zac. But Zac is only a boy.

Among coughs and shuffles, Erica joins the crowd late, pushing her mobile into the deep pockets of her dungarees. Some of her curls have come loose round the ears and blow across her face. And then I notice something: the way my mother looks at her.

Some kind of change spreads over Mum's face and her mouth tightens. I've seen it happen before; she suspects something.

Mr Johnston catches Mum's eye and turns on the spot, pushing his way roughly through the huddled assembly and stomping back to the school cabin.

Harvey raises his eyebrows. So does Mum. Zac stares at the ground.

What on earth is happening? It's as if the whole world knows what's going on.

Except me.

CHAPTER SIXTEEN

ERICA

'Will, the sooner you get back here, the better. Harvey is doing his best, but... I know... It was just obvious to me that... yes, see, I was thinking the same. She's worked for all sorts of charities before, hasn't she? Did you say she'd done some work for the Wildlife Trust? Yes, but... don't you think it's at least possible? She'd have press contacts, surely...'

I can hardly breathe. My right ear is firmly pressed against the wall between my room and the living room. My father on the other end of the line is obviously on a rant of some sort, but soon Mum cuts in again.

'The other one who was acting weird was Roger Johnston. When Harvey asked the question, he just turned round and left. Couldn't look any of us in the eye.'

No. No no no! You've got it all wrong! I want to shout it out loud, but I can't.

How can I tell them that the one they're looking for is a 12-year-old boy? Zac's probably so keen to save us all from nature's wrath, he'll stop at nothing to derail our building project!

It feels weird beyond belief to carry on exactly as we are, but that's what we do. We eat. We sleep. We go to the pier and meet the supply boat. We open tins and go to school and do homework and Skype with grandparents. It's so strange, the way that we're all part of this big conspiracy not to say a thing about what happened, even when Dad arrives back with a couple of investigators from the National Wildlife Crime Unit. They visit the school to interview everyone about what happened in the storehouse and Mr Johnston turns on the hyper-enthusiastic-about-wildlife-voice just to impress them.

I wonder. Maybe Mum's right after all. Oh, I don't know.

Zac basically communicates with me in sighs and grunts. But I've had enough; I'd rather be a loner than a beggar. Who knows—maybe at some point he'll be sick of the hermit life—too late then, ha. We'll see who does the grovelling then.

Mr Johnston has the grace not to say anything when I move my seat to the corner of the table. I'd rather face the wall than sit opposite him anymore. For all I care, Zac can sulk till Kingdom come.

Mr Johnston is being a bit strange, too. He's been really absent-minded lately; and Struan and his table get away with murder when our teacher normally comes down on them like twenty tons of bricks. My brother can't believe his luck and whistles all the way home.

'School's kind of fun just now, isn't it?' he offers.

I could have ignored him.

I *should* have ignored him—after all, he is only eight. Still, it's kind of satisfying to feel his shin crunch under the impact of my boot—so satisfying, in fact, that I don't even care about being grounded and sent to bed early after a thirteen-minute lecture (I timed it) on the responsibility that comes with being a big sister and how my parents have a lot on their plate just now.

Whose dim idea was it anyway, to move to this stupid island with a bunch of idiots?

I'm a bit wound up, and the best way to deal with that is training my eyes on the horizon and trying to relax. I can just about catch the whole coast from here—the pier and the cove with the beach, some of the other huts and, if I crane my neck to the very right, the Ben, still with a tiny dusting of snow at the top. It helps. Not that it lets me make sense of it all, but it dissolves some of my anger and makes me feel small, in a good way. The clouds line up for sunset and I breathe deeply, letting the light, the rhythm of the sea and the ripple of the machair work their magic on my troubled mind.

Hey. Wait a minute. What's that? I shake my head to

focus and peer more closely. There's someone out there, in the half-light—it's Erica! What is she doing out at this time of night?

All across our little settlement, curtains are being drawn, computers switched on, dishes washed. *Why is she heading towards the Ben? Hang on—is that a man up there by the trees? Is he waiting for her?*

I can't believe it—it looks like Mum was right. *What do I do?*

I'm grounded, I'm perfectly aware of that. I also understand that my parents will probably not give me pocket money for the next hundred years and that I won't get within a mile of the computer again in my lifetime, but even that doesn't matter now. Erica is meeting someone in secret and that can only mean one thing. I grab my phone to take pictures as evidence. Finally, Dad will be proud of me and once the informer is gone, we'll make progress at last. Looks like Zac's not the traitor after all. I'd feel some regret for suspecting him if he hadn't been such a complete idiot lately.

Without another thought, I climb onto my tiny fold-down desk and squeeze through the open window. And while above us, the clouds draw together like curtains, I follow the two shadows at a distance.

CHAPTER SEVENTEEN

SPY

It takes me a while to get close; it's tricky, keeping up and staying out of sight all at the same time. It becomes even harder when the two figures leave the path and cut along the top of a steep slope westwards, towards the more exposed part of the island. Is there a boat, tied up by the cliffs, waiting to take the mystery man back to the mainland and his news desk?

I'm disgusted with Erica—the bare-faced cheek of the whole thing is what I can't get over. She must know people are suspicious of her. I wonder if she's been bribed. She only took this job because she needed the money; I heard her say so myself. The amount of trouble she's got Dad into! And he still won't hear a word against her. Well, if she thinks she can just put everyone's career at risk for a quick buck, she can think again.

I have to get evidence of this secret meeting, then I'll have proof that she's the informer—imagine how relieved everyone will be. Mum and Dad will be so pleased.

Step by step up the hill, the low light lulls me into a twilight daze.

Hey! Where have they gone?

The terrain is stony and uneven now that we've passed the trees. Below me, the waves crash onto the rocks, sending sea-spray high into the air, but I can't see the two figures anywhere.

For goodness' sake; I've managed to lose them! Why am I so useless?

As I check my surroundings, a new thought creeps into my imagination. Even at this moment, *they* could be watching *me*.

Are they dangerous? I've probably watched too many thrillers, but who knows what else Erica's capable of? Not to mention the man. I peer down over the cliffs where wet rocks glisten. It would be very easy to make a fall look like an accident here. I think of Zac's wacky wilderness theory and feel a little faint.

I need to get out of here, before it's too late. But wait, there's something in the distance, just above the cliff-face ahead. A tiny flicker of light, but it's enough.

I tiptoe towards the opening of a cave, wide enough at the entrance for a small fire. Looking back over my shoulder confirms that, no—this won't be visible from the huts, we've gone too far round the Ben and all I can see from here is the bottomless, merciless Atlantic Ocean.

I freeze as fragments of speech drift from the cave, warped by the wind and distorted by my fear. If I'm quick, and precise, I can take advantage of my one trump card: surprise.

Don't rush now, plenty of time for that later. I edge my way along the cliff ledge towards the cave. Carefully, I retrieve my phone from my pocket, switch it to mute and set the camera. I place my finger on the button and mentally mark out an escape route through the twilight.

If I stretch my arm into the opening of the cave I can take a picture… yes, that's better than showing myself— and it may give me the edge. I bet I'd outrun Erica easily enough, but if the news-hound turns out to be a sprinter, I'm in trouble.

The more I think about it, the more likely I am to mess it up.

Here goes…

Arm extended.

Camera pointed.

Lull in conversation.

Have they spotted me?

Click. Flash.

And then I run, pushing the phone into my coat pocket as I scramble along the cliff edge, using my left hand to steady myself against the slope. I stumble, twice, as if roots were shooting out of the ground to trip me up. I hear voices raised behind me, but the hostile howl of the wind is enough to swallow any noise, both their screams and mine. It slows me on my way as I push on through the moorland back to the trees. Finally, just as the moon appears in the sky, I emerge and sprint the last stretch downhill and onto the square. It's eerily quiet as I catch my breath.

Back through the window?

No. I'll walk right through the door.

With my head held high.

My parents are speechless when they answer my forceful knock.

But they are even more speechless when, squashed together on the futon, I reveal the crucial evidence.

I watch their reaction rather than the phone screen. There is a tightness in both their faces. *Have I messed up again? Is it too dark? Too blurry? Too shocking, perhaps?*

Before I get to ask any of these, my parents do the very, very last thing I expected them to do.

They burst out laughing.

What the...

Hard, loud, tear-wet laughter. Mum throws herself back into the futon and wipes her eyes; Dad places my phone on the table and rocks noiselessly as he does when he really loses it, holding his stomach.

'That explains a few things,' squeaks Mum. Dad can only nod in that jerky way.

I snatch the phone which has already gone back to screensaver. Tapping the button, a photo appears. At least the image is in focus: that's Erica, a hand round her windswept hair... *Hang on. That's not her hand, that's Mr...*

WHAT?

WHAAAT? Eew!

Mr Johnston and Erica are in the picture, embracing. And kissing. On the mouth.

'That's not even funny, that's disgusting!' I snap.

My mother's arm creeps around my shoulder. I try to elbow her away, but instead I'm pulled into a tight, family hug.

So tight that I can't help smiling myself.

CHAPTER EIGHTEEN

NEWS

The next morning, I avoid eye contact with Mr Johnston at all costs. I hand him my homework while staring at my shoes, collect the jotters up as if my hands were particularly interesting, and when my eyes finally do flit up, I find that he, too, is looking away. Fancy a man of that age being embarrassed. Why am *I* blushing bright red? As if *I* had anything to be embarrassed about.

I just wish I could spread the gossip a bit, but the only vaguely trustworthy, old-enough-to-understand-the-grossness-of-it person is still sulking. I nearly fall off my chair when Zac speaks to me: friendly, casual and as if nothing had happened at all.

'Hey, Em. What's up with Johnston? He's being a bit strange today, don't you think?'

It's a start, but no way am I going to let him see how desperately I need his friendship right now. I bury my nose in our reading book about dolphins.

Zac pokes his pencil into my book and I look up in

outrage. 'Hey!'

'Em, look. I'm sorry. I'm just worried that I'm right. I want you to *believe* me, but that doesn't mean I actually want it to be *true*, OK?'

I shuffle in my seat. 'All right.'

'And...' he says with a wicked, wicked grin on his face, 'I can tell *you* know what's up with Johnston.'

I crack and smile back at him. 'Talk to you at break,' I whisper as Mr Johnston hands us two test papers and takes the dolphin books away.

Dad is still uncharacteristically cheerful at the table at night-time. They stopped work slightly early as the wind was picking up, but I don't think that's the reason.

'You obviously like a good love affair, eh?' I tease, but he shakes his head.

'Dinner!' shouts Mum from the front door and seconds later, Struan bursts in, covered in sticky weeds, heather and sand.

'Back outside while I dust you down.' Mum reaches for the broom and mock-scrubs my brother who bends to avoid the worst tickles.

'Struan dancing,' points Izzy, and we all laugh.

The breeze carries a couple of leaves through the window and Mum shuts it, still laughing.

I square up to Dad. 'OK! This isn't like our family! What's up?'

'I've had a bit of good news.'

Mum beams at him across the table as he continues. 'The company did an investigation and they've found the informer. Turns out it was Dr Ian Pratt himself, trying to discredit me and get me fired from the project. He was trying to portray me as a thug who wilfully ruins the environment. But then they found an email trail between him and the news agency, as well as the pictures on his computer. So all he got was the sack himself. My heart bleeds for him!'

Dad pulls the saddest grimace he can muster and winks at me.

But that means...

'What does that mean?' Struan asks.

Zac and Erica and Mr Johnston were not to blame.

'It means, Oh Struan-of-little-brain, that *I-am-a-prat* won't be back, and we'll get a better architect. It means that Dad's all right. And it means no more hassle.' I love lecturing my brother and do my best to make my voice sound as if I am talking to a baby.

The next moment, we all scream as a huge gust of wind howls through our house. There is a loud rumble and the hut shakes a little. A split-second later, the roof caves in with a crash and I am lying on my back on the floor.

The first thought that crosses my mind is: *I'm cold.*

The next is: *How come there's a tree in our living room?*

CHAPTER NINETEEN

TRUTH

I wrap my hands around the mug. It's what a mug should be, thick and solid. I pull the blanket closer.

'The air ambulance is on its way. The wind seems to be settling, so hopefully they'll get through all right. I think we must be jinxed or something!' Dad curses under his breath.

Mum is over at Petra's hut which is close beside ours and got the worst of the tree. It landed right on Anna's bedroom. It always surprises me, but Mum can be quite good in a crisis—as long as it's not *our* crisis. She just handed me Izzy and climbed over the branches to the kitchen cupboard where the first aid box is. We should have left immediately, I guess, but Snarl's cage was bent by the impact, and what does that stupid rodent do? Escape, that's what.

'I'm not leaving without Snarl!'

'Struan…'

But my heart softens when I see his face. We spend

a pretty unpleasant hour crawling through what's left of my brother's room before discovering the fugitive inside Struan's chanter bag.

Finally, we arrive at Muriel and Harvey's. 'Poor Anna,' I whisper to Zac. 'I wouldn't fancy a helicopter trip all the way to hospital in Glasgow, but I guess…'

'Yeah, better safe than sorry. What if she's really hurt her spine?' He looks at me darkly.

'They're probably just keeping her still as a precaution. At least Petra is going, too. She'll want her mum with her.'

I regret every last nasty thought I've had about Anna, curling myself up in the corner and listening to wind's soulful song. I'm woken by the chopper, but I don't feel refreshed. Dad's face looks wrinklier than I remember it when he steps out to meet the paramedics.

'Sorry, took longer to get here than we expected. We had a bit of trouble landing. Stupid seagulls kept flying at us. Took us about four attempts. Where's the patient?'

Immediately, the adults bustle to Anna's hut, but Zac's eyes bore into me.

I know what he's waiting for.

Pulling my hoodie up close around my neck, I give in: 'I guess you may be onto something. Happy?'

I don't look back as I stride away and wait until I've rounded the corner to Petra's hut, before wiping cold sweat off my forehead.

What if it's true?
What if the wilderness really is against us?
Dizzy, I steady myself against the metal of the door.
We don't stand a chance.

CHAPTER TWENTY

SUMMER

Amazing, what summer can do.

The swaying machair bursts with wildflowers and puffins with bright beaks dive into crystal-blue wave-crests. From the higher vantage points on the island, Zac and I often spot sun-lit seals swimming gracefully underwater, clearly visible against the bright coral of the seabed.

Izzy has started running everywhere. The workers, too, have made excellent progress in the good weather and their hard work is beginning to show. Like any of Dad's projects, the prep has taken so long that it almost catches me by surprise when the walls of the main hotel building shoot up from the ground. The little hunting lodge on the other side of the Ben is nearly finished already. Dad says that all the exteriors have to be done before the winter storms. I feel nervous at the thought of more bad weather—more storms; it's the last thing we need. It took ages for the two new shiny cabins to arrive to replace our tree-damaged ones. It'll take much longer to cut that moment from my memory.

The list of mishaps is never far from my mind and images of sinking containers, rats, splintered trunks, and above all, gulls, haunt my thoughts.

Even *I* don't have faith enough for all of this to be coincidence. I can't believe I didn't see it before. Zac is right; we are under attack.

The realisation is so raw it's making me paranoid: every blade of grass is a lethal sling, every pebble a missile, every root a claw.

Being frightened is exhausting.

With a groan, I sink into my chair by the school stove on Monday morning.

'Hey.' Zac throws his bag on the floor. 'Have you tried to talk to them?'

'Yep.'

He leans forward. 'No success?'

'Nope.' I slide my jacket of and throw it over the back of my chair.

He sighs. 'Don't take it personally, Em, my parents don't buy it either. That's the hassle with not being an adult. No-one cares what we think.'

'Tell me about it.'

I rehearsed my speech all yesterday morning, waited for the right moment and put our theory to Mum while she was changing Izzy's nappy. There was a fair bit of ah-ing and hm-hm-ing. I asked what she thought and she looked at me. 'Sorry, darling, I was only half listening. What was all that again?'

Mr Johnston clears his throat, as he does every school morning at nine o'clock. *Wish I could get the picture of the kiss out of my head.* At least they aren't secretive anymore. I saw them yesterday walking along the east beach, holding hands. Mum thinks it's cute.

'Morning all. Please get your jotters out, everyone, we're starting with writing. For the younger ones...'

I zone out until I hear my name. And here it comes.

'Zac and Em, you haven't done a substantial piece of creative writing since you got here. Not personal writing, not reflection; this time it's creative. That means a story. So, as we're busy with field study later in the week, I'll give you a chance to get started in class today. A week today, I want it to be finished. Make it the best you can: introduce the key players, build up the tension nicely, finish with some kind of dramatic event and round the story off with a satisfying ending after.'

Whoa, hold on. My pencil races across the page as I take all this down.

'Word count?' Zac asks.

'At least 700.'

'HOW much? You must be joking!' Zac splutters. 'Mr Johnston, that's more than we've ever written before.

That's tons!'

'Yeah, that's way more than…' I begin, but our teacher cuts me short.

'I don't want to hear it. Don't waste your breath, you two—put your energy into an idea. You've got till break to get started. After that we'll sort out the practicalities of the field trip.'

Mr Johnston has already turned his back to give Struan's whole table a rollicking for giggling. If he's still embarrassed that the whole island knows about his love life thanks to me, he doesn't show it.

'Any ideas?' I whisper. Zac shakes his head and stares out to sea.

With every passing second, I feel my throat tighten.

With every passing minute, the blank page beneath my hand looks emptier.

Time passes. I feel beads of sweat forming on my forehead as, opposite me, Zac's pencil begins to scratch.

What's he writing?

My heart races, but my mind stays vacant, right until the bell for break.

'All right, everyone. The pairs and trios we're working in are on the board. We'll head out, all of us together, and each group will focus on a different aspect of wildlife here on Skelsay. That may mean splitting up—some on the beach, some in the cove on the northern side, some on the Ben—you get the idea.'

I glance at the board. I thought Zac and I would have been paired with the younger ones, but we're meant to be looking at birds of prey on the Ben. *So far so good, but...*

Zac voices exactly what I'm thinking. 'Mr Johnson, are you planning to let the younger ones go to the beach on their own? Anna is only just back from hospital. Shouldn't she be careful?'

'All protective, are you?' Our teacher dismisses him with a chuckle. 'Let me do the worrying about health and safety, Zac. You just spot an eagle or two and I'll be happy. They'll be all right—I'm never going to be far away.'

'But...'

'Any other questions about the trip?' says Mr Johnson slightly too cheerfully for my liking.

'Yeah!' booms my brother. 'Do we get to take beach toys?'

His suggestion is met with huge approval from his gang.

'Tempting as it may be—no.' Mr Johnston's ears redden. 'That's not quite the attitude I was hoping for.'

'What *are* we going to do then?'

Struan's question sounds like an accusation and the tone isn't lost on Mr Johnston, king of sarcasm.

'Thank goodness, Struan, I thought you were never

going to ask. You've got your nature diaries, haven't you? With plenty of blank pages for sketching and writing down your observations. Which means sitting still...'

Several of the boys whinge loudly.

'...and listening to what's going on around you.'

Struan snorts.

Mr Johnston smiles. 'You take notes on what you see, draw sketches into your diaries, including mapping any nest or den locations. The cliffs above the beach are well worth looking at for nesting seabirds, for example. Those of you who can take camera phones are welcome to use those, too. I expect you to copy and describe any tracks or faeces...'

'What?' I whisper.

'Poo,' mutters Zac, clearly enough for all to hear.

'Ah. Why didn't he say poo?' comments Struan loudly.

'Finally, each group will prepare a talk and present their findings. If we can, we'll do this outside; it seems appropriate. You have two days. Hopefully you'll all have lots to share.' Our teacher's face glows. 'I look forward to your discoveries.'

I, on the other hand, feel sick.

Zac and I need to talk.

And quickly.

CHAPTER TWENTY-ONE

JOHNSTON

We wait.

I cast an anxious glance at our hut, but Mum is still painting, so I'm safe for the moment. She always forgets everything around her when she paints.

Finally, Struan emerges from the school hut after his attitude-induced detention. I can hear him, even from here.

'See you tomorrow, Mr Johnson. Sure, I'll give Mum the note.'

As soon as the door closes, my brother dashes towards the cliffs, folds something into a paper aeroplane and lets the wind carry it out to sea from his hand. The greedy waves devour it in an instant.

'Now.' Zac and I step out of our hiding place beside the storehouse and jog towards the school hut.

'At least we know he's still in there…' I gasp as I pull the door open and realise I should have knocked. Our teacher is there, but so is Erica, sitting cross-legged on the desk by the stove.

My desk!

Zac recovers first. 'Ahem. Sorry, sir. We were wondering if we could have a word. please?'

Mr Johnston scratches behind his ear, a sure sign he is irritated. 'Well, to be honest, I'd rather wait till tomorrow. It's been a bit of a long day and I've still got to sort out some bits and pieces for the field trip. Can it wait?' His voice is pleasant enough, but his eyes stay steely.

'Come on,' I mutter, but Zac acts as if he hasn't heard me.

'No,' he says.

Erica laughs, taking me completely by surprise. She shakes her hair back and her eyes twinkle.

'Och, Roger, just humour them a minute. I don't mind, honestly. It won't take that long, I'm sure.'

He smiles at her, his caterpillar eyebrows arched, and turns back to us. 'All right then. And this better be good.'

There is silence. Only minutes ago, we decided there was no way around it, we'd have to make him listen, or someone would get hurt on that trip. Hurt, or worse. Now it seems impossible to even begin. But I have no choice. *Here goes...*

'Mr Johnston, try to think of all the things that have gone wrong since we got here.'

I leave a little moment for his mind to do the work: a container crashing into the sea, an air ambulance, dead rats, a blizzard, a tree trunk snapped like a match and skewering out cabins. Maybe he knows of more.

Erica has stopped smiling.

'Well, Zac here and I, we sort of have this theory. It sounds a bit far-fetched. And ridiculous. Not to mention kind of impossible, but we are wondering if…'

My courage deserts me, but Zac is ready to step in.

'We reckon that the wilderness is against us—here on Skelsay, anyway.'

Erica is smiling again, and so is our teacher. Not the reaction Zac was hoping for.

'PLEASE! This is not a joke. We're actually quite worried, especially with this field trip…'

'Zac,' interrupts Mr Johnston calmly. 'I am the first to agree with you that nature, awesome as it is, needs to be respected. I agree that there are dangers as well as thrills. Saying that, do I believe that the wilderness is our enemy? Most certainly not.'

I burst out: 'But what if it's the other way around?'

'Explain, Em.'

'I mean,' I say quietly, listening to the waves pounding the shore in the distance. 'What if the enemy is us? We started it.'

The door flies open and we all jump at least a little.

Struan wipes his nose on his sleeve. 'There you are! Mum sent me; tea's in five minutes. Hey—why are you back at school? Are you in trouble, too?'

'I'm just coming.' I frown at my brother.

'Remember to come dressed properly for the field trip tomorrow,' says Mr Johnston, turning away and busying himself in the book corner. We are dismissed.

It takes a second to sink in.

Failure.

I eat my dinner in silence and go to bed early, looking out waterproofs and walking boots and charging my phone overnight.

I'm no psychic, but I know tomorrow will be a disaster.

And this time I'll make sure we have the photos to prove it.

CHAPTER TWENTY-TWO

SCREE

'Struan, behave yourself today, will you? Are you sure that you're allowed to bring those beach toys?' Mum shoots me a glance of bewildered stress. 'Em, keep an eye on him, OK? I don't like the idea of Struan let loose on his own.' My brother is busy inflating a plastic shark, or else he would have protested.

'You and me both. But actually, Mum, I'm not even in Struan's group. The little ones are going to the shore.'

Mum stops. 'So, what about you?'

'Zac and I are heading up the Ben to see birds of prey.'

'The hiiills are aliiiiive…' sings Struan, opera style, emerging from behind his shark.

Mum doesn't pay attention to him though. 'What, by yourselves, Em?'

'Yep.' My answers get shorter, a fact not lost on my mother who knows the tell-tale signs of my nerves.

'That seems a bit risky to me,' she states cautiously. 'No adults?'

'Nope.'

The weird thing is: I said exactly the same thing myself. But now that it comes from Mum, I'm annoyed. It probably comes through in my slightly edgy tone. 'We'll be fine, Mum; we can look after ourselves. Nothing to worry about, eh, Struan?'

Struan nods vigorously.

Apart from the fact that the whole of Skelsay is out to get us.

Struan storms ahead, the inflatable shark tucked under his arm.

Mr Johnston is already waiting outside the school hut, ticking off names on a list. His jacket is tied around his waist; it's dry, even warm. The three groups separate out as more of us arrive.

'Rule number one: be careful. Take care and be mindful of your surroundings—the sea, cliff edges, slopes of scree—all can be dangerous environments—always err on the side of caution. Em and Zac, you'll need to be really, really careful in that wind. Avoid the steepest part at the end, please. I'll obviously watch the youngest group myself.'

My brother's face falls.

'And what on earth is that, Struan? I said NO toys! Anyway, the rest of you will be on your own. As far as you can, stay within shouting distance. Do not go further than the limit on your instruction card. Got it?'

Everyone nods, most solemnly. Zac and I exchange a tense look.

'We'll meet back here in an hour and a half for the first debrief.' Mr Johnston's trousers flutter in the wind. 'All right? Off you go then. Hey, Struan—wait, no rushing off! Remember, I'm going with your group. And why have you brought your chanter?'

'I might be bored.'

'You're going to scare off any wildlife. That thing can be heard from quite a distance.' Mr Johnston sounds exasperated.

'That thing can be heard in China,' whispers Zac, so that only I can hear it. I laugh harder than I probably should.

We are joined by Anna and Catriona for the first part of our way, up the slope to the trees. Along with Gregor, they'll study the flower variety on the machair. Not exactly taxing, but probably to go easy on Anna's bruised back. When they turn off towards the east shore, flower press in hand, we begin to climb up the side of the Ben. There's no real path yet, just deer trails through the bracken. The heather is beginning to turn purple and the last of the yellow gorse blossom has faded. Below us, the azure sea stretches as far as the cornflower-blue sky. I wipe my brow. *Only two years, and there will be a funicular railway right here. No-one will be sweating then.*

'When you see it like this it's hard to imagine that there's anything wrong, isn't it?' I ask.

Zac's face is grim. 'Watch, OK? That's all I'm saying.'

Just then, a huge shape rises above us; its gentle wingbeats casting a shadow over the rocks further up the hill.

'Oh wow! Zac, look, up there—do you see it?' I gasp. 'It's a golden eagle; I can make out the tail quite easily.'

He lifts his binoculars to his eyes while I try to sketch the shape of the raptor, which is hard when it keeps disappearing and then gliding back into view.

'Hang on, is it coming down?'

He's right; the bird has plummeted, skimming over the rocks above. Zac points. 'I think it's got something. A rabbit?'

'Could be...'

We stand, spellbound by the elegance with which the giant bird approaches, as it veers left and makes for a crack in the rocks above. Without even realising, I have held my breath. In slow motion, Zac hands me the binoculars—the last thing we want to do is startle the animal.

As I focus the lenses, a strange calm comes over me: I am breathing the same air as this majestic creature. I can't control its wildness, but for now, I have become a secret witness of its world. I am almost giddy with the thrill. For the first time in my life, I can imagine why people might take up bird-watching.

'Zac! Zac, there's a chick there, I think.' Yes, that is definitely the fluffy head of a chick—just one—its hooked beak tearing blood-red strips from its breakfast. I should be disgusted, but I feel elated instead.

I can barely take it in: the sunlit slopes, the wind singing in the cracks, and this beautiful, graceful, merciless hunter.

'An eaglet,' whispers Zac.

The fluffy chick in the distance feebly moves its featherless wings up and down and there is a tugging at my soul, so strong it almost hurts. Spellbound, we stand and watch.

'We're *so* lucky, Zac.'

The adult eagle swings itself into the air once more, passing us overhead, and soars towards the clouds. Its feathers glow gold, matching its yellow talons and beak. With every heavy wingbeat, the feather fingers at the end of each wing spread out wide. We watch until we can't see it any more. I become aware of the wind, still tearing at our clothes.

'How long have we got?' Zac wants to know.

I wriggle my watch out from under my sleeve. 'We should probably start heading down in twenty minutes, I reckon.'

'What do you say we get a closer-up picture of the

chick?' Zac is as windswept as I am, but there is a weird gleam in his eyes that wasn't there before.

'Well…' I try to judge the distance to nest, high above us. 'Maybe we could make it up there. But I'm not that great with heights, Zac. And what about this war with the wilderness, huh?'

Zac doesn't waver. 'It looks OK around here. I can't see any danger as long as we're careful on the slope.'

I bite my lip. *Wow, it's steep.* 'Can you even climb up scree?'

'There's only one way to find out.'

Little avalanches of scree slide beneath each of his strides.

'We have to climb fast if we want to make it back for the meeting with the others,' I shout upwards.

'You better get a move on then,' Zac replies. He doesn't even look back, which is a bit odd.

My feet slip with every step and I struggle to keep up with him.

'Come on, Em. We've got to hurry a bit,' Zac pants. 'Unless you want to be around when Birdzilla comes back.'

Faster, I scurry up the hill after him, using both hands and feet to scramble over the stones. I push the image of strong talons, that horrible hooked beak and a two-metre wingspan from my increasingly anxious mind.

At one point I'm convinced I hear shouting, faint and distant.

'Did you hear that?' I call to Zac, who is only a little ahead of me. The wind is deafening. He shrugs. *What does that mean? He hasn't heard anything? He has, but doesn't care? Or that he hasn't understood me in the first place? What's wrong with him today?*

Nearing the eyrie, I catch up as he hesitates. 'Let's go sideways,' I suggest. 'That way we can get a decent shot without going too close and disturbing it.'

'Getting close is the whole point,' says Zac with conviction. But I notice that his watchful eyes are on the sky as much as on the way ahead.

The next thirty seconds feel like an hour—every foothold is a potential fall. Far below, our classmates are mere dots on the machair and every sound becomes the screech of an angry eagle to my anxious mind. Finally, we are there, diagonally above the chick. I swallow hard. The slope looks much, much, MUCH steeper when you look at it from here.

'Go on,' says Zac, gesturing towards my phone.

'Oh. Yes. All right!' For a moment, I'm mesmerised by the innocence of the cute mottled bundle of fluff, with its beady eyes and oversized hooked beak. It's so hard to imagine the sleek hunter it will become one day. I focus the camera. The chick observes us with interest.

Click. And again.

A sudden, head-splitting shriek and angry wings startle me. The beast is upon us, flying at us from all directions. In that split second, I'm back on the ferry with the gulls and the fear paralyses me.

'Em, get down! DOWN!'

I obey, ducking and clutching on to the scree to steady myself.

'This way! It's easier to go up than down!' I can hear the panic in his voice.

'Can't we slide down?' I yell at him, while ducking another flyover. But this time I do feel the sharp scratch of talons on my neck and the pain is so intense that I can't help but arch my body backwards.

Which kind of makes the decision for me. The loose stones beneath my feet give way and I skid, clutching my bleeding neck, into the void below.

About a million pieces of rock keep me company as I scream.

CHAPTER TWENTY-THREE

SKY

Why is there blood in my mouth, crunchy blood?

I try to spit, but even that minute movement takes more energy than I can summon. I want to sleep, but there are voices, distant and dreamy, calling my name. *Sleep.*

'Come on! Quickly!'

Why can't they let me sleep? Do I know that voice? I'm not sure. It doesn't matter. Nothing matters.

'Help me, someone! Over here! Em, can you hear me? EM!'

Something is touching my head. Then my shoulders, squeezing hard.

I wish they'd leave me alone.

'Don't move her. Wait till the helicopter gets here; just in case.'

I try to open my eyes but only one will open, just a crack.

'She's trying to open her eyes—thank God, thank GOD!'

I feel someone's breath on my face. I wish I could remember who that voice belongs to.

'Here. Try that, but gently. They won't be long.'

I jerk as the cold water runs over my face and my eyes are gently wiped of dust and grit. A fuzzy outline comes into view.

My father's face.

What... How did he... How long have I...

Like a whip, comprehension cracks through my mind.

'Zac,' I stammer and struggle upwards.

'Hey, hey, hey, take it easy. Zac? He came down the other side and got help. He's got a nasty gash on his head, but he'll be fine. Lie still now, the paramedics are on their way.'

I'm forced down, a rolled-up jacket beneath my head.

'Yeah, you're not the only one who's had a rough day.' Erica's grinning face pops out over my father's shoulder. 'I'm telling you, it might just be the last field trip Roger ever runs. He's just about had it.'

I close my eyes again as a new wave of nausea muddies my mind. *Maybe I could have a rest now, sleep—then I'll feel better.*

Dad pinches my cheek. 'No, Em, we need to keep you alert. We don't know if there is internal bleeding yet. Stay with us, darling, not long now. Open your eyes, keep them open; that's it.'

I ignore him and let my lids droop.

Erica is still there. 'Hey, do you want to know about the others? Little Mikey and your brother?'

I open my eyes again, as far as I can. My body moulds itself uncomfortably into its rocky bed, but at least I'm listening.

'Good girl, I know it's not easy for you.' Dad just keeps on stroking my forehead while Erica talks and talks. Her voice is cheerful, but also a bit forced.

'Well, those wee boys are rascals anyway, but they went right up to the seal colony on the sand bank. You should never approach a seal when it has young. Roger had left them collecting shells while he checked on the middle group, but he didn't get far by the time he heard their screams. Did you know that seal bites can be really dangerous? It's all those bugs they have in their mouths—you can catch nasty infections from that. Your brother's leg is a bit of a mess.'

I hear the chopper in the distance, but blood is rushing so loudly in my ears that I don't bother turning my head. Erica is still rambling on—something about snakes and ladders—or is it adders?—and rocks.

The chopper lands, strangers' voices speak to Dad and Erica and—finally—me. Strange hands lift me onto a strange stretcher and the sun's warm rays caress me to sleep as I drift off, lifted up into the sky, or to heaven; I don't much care which.

CHAPTER TWENTY-FOUR

RELAX

Three days later, we are travelling again. My brother has barely stopped talking for the whole journey.

"Shh, Struan!' I whisper. After all, we're not alone. Dad came down to fetch us all: Struan and Mikey, pumped full of antibiotics and their wounds covered in antiseptic. Then there's Gregor with his adder bite, for which he had to get some sort of antidote, and his mum. And then there's me. Dad calls me his rainbow girl, multi-coloured with all my bruising. But no broken bones. My left eye still won't open fully and the scratches on the back of my neck hurt like hell, but they reckon there is nothing *seriously* wrong.

In the car mirror, it's easy to inspect the walking wounded unnoticed. We're soldiers in a war we didn't choose, but they don't even know it.

As we head, unstoppably, back to the battlefield, worry whittles away at my mind until sleep wins.

When our boat pulls in, there's a little crowd waiting at the pier. I can see Zac, and a haggard-looking Mr Johnston. Erica stands beside him, her arm tucked under his. My mother hugs me so hard I can barely breathe.

'Hey, Mum.'

She bites back tears. Struan is already showing off his bandaged leg to anyone who will look and delighting anyone who will listen with tales of his trauma.

I walk towards our hut, nodding to Zac on the way, with Izzy running after me as fast as her wee legs will carry her. As I pass the building site, I am struck by the progress they've made since we first arrived. The walls stand, like a giant maze, waiting for the roof constructions that are being assembled on the mainland.

I close the hut door behind me and feel glad to be back home. Izzy wrestles her wellies off on the floor, Struan and Dad sink onto the futon and Mum puts the kettle on.

I know I should wait for the right moment, but I can't; I just can't hold it in anymore.

'Right. This time I'm going to make sure that you listen to me. Really listen. Struan, just let me finish, OK? It's important. I've tried to tell you before, though it *is* hard to believe, and it sounds a bit dramatic, but now I'm certain: We really *are* at war with this island. Or, this island, this wilderness, is at war with *us*.'

Dad is looking away, no doubt thinking of a clever argument to dismiss what I'm saying. Mum subtly shakes her head.

'I'm NOT finished yet!' I yell. 'Think of all the stuff that's gone wrong since we got here—come on, Dad, you must have been thinking it too, on the journey. As soon as Skelsay came into view! I saw that look on your face.'

'Em, you've got to realise...' starts Mum in her *I'm-going-to-keep-calm-even-amid-all-this-provocation* voice.

I roll my eyes.

'...that we've been around a bit longer than you. Dad's been involved in lots of projects. Some easy, and some *not* so easy. This one is *not* so easy. I know you've had a fright with that fall, and it's only natural to look for an explanation, but that doesn't mean there is anything dodgy or sinister going on. Accidents happen. Relax.'

She smooths my hair, but I pull away. 'Relax. *Relax?* *Accidents happen?* I almost *died!* Is that the best you've got?' I screech. 'Struan was attacked by a seal—*attacked!*'

'Mum's right, Em.' Dad interrupts my rant. 'Let's not overreact here. We obviously need to be careful and responsible, but the idea that something is out to get us is just...'

'Just what? Impossible? Mad? *Crazy?*' I shout with my good eye bulging out of its socket.

Dad stops and leaves his unfinished sentence hanging

there, like a soggy sock on the washing line. He doesn't meet my eye either.

Struan however, stares at me, 'At war? Are you serious?' he breathes.

Mum sighs theatrically. 'Now see what you've done. I know it's been a rough few days for you, but don't freak out the other kids. Roger Johnston has a hard-enough job already, keeping all of you under control; I don't want him to have to deal with this scaremongering as well. Em?'

Somehow, Mum can always tell when I'm only half-listening, which is beyond irritating.

'Whatever,' I snap, grabbing my bag and heading for my room.

I need a plan. And fast.

CHAPTER TWENTY-FIVE

FACT

None of us really know what to say to Mr Johnston as we push and hobble through the door of the school hut. Any chatter is subdued, apart from my brother's, of course, who has drawn a comic of the seal attack (*When Seals Go Bad*) and copied it on Dad's scanner. Two pounds each seems a bit steep to me, but there's no shortage of takers.

'How are you feeling, Em?' says Zac, not looking straight at me.

I try to give him a smile but smiling hurts. The more spectacular colours on my bruises are only coming out now. I've avoided mirrors as much as I could, but now and again you can't help catching a glimpse. *I'd* look away if I was him.

'Look, don't answer that. Stupid question. I just wanted to say... Em, I am so sorry. *I* made you climb up there. I did.'

'Don't worry, I'm fine, honestly.'

135

'No, really. We knew all along it was dangerous, and I was *still* stupid enough to take a risk.'

'You're right about one thing,' I say as I take my pencil case out. 'We've known all along, and I don't know how much time we've got. I tried to tell my parents, again. But they won't buy it, even now.'

'Well, if the adults don't want to listen, maybe the children will,' he says solemnly. 'I think it's time we warned the little ones.'

I glance over.

These kids are dim enough to pay Struan £2 for a home-made comic. Really, do we want them on our side?

Mr Johnston clears his throat. 'Right, class, we better make a start. There is something I need to say, right from the off, and it's this.' He looks out of the window and takes a big breath. 'I truly regret how the field trip worked out, and I blame no-one but myself for it. I made a bad call to send you out on your own. Leaving you unattended… That was irresponsible. I should have known to take the risks more seriously.'

There isn't even a hint of a spark in his eyes.

'That said, I'm delighted to welcome back Struan, Mikey, Gregor and Em from Glasgow.'

Struan raises his hands in triumph and waves like a winning athlete. Mr Johnston ignores him and continues. 'We're all relieved that you're safe now, but for me the bottom line is this: you could have *died*.'

A different kind of silence falls. Not the lazy, barely-listening absence of talking. A treacly kind of tension trickles in and sticks. No-one seems to feel like speaking anymore. A comic slides off Struan's desk and glides in zigzags to the floor, but no-one even looks at it. All eyes are on Mr Johnston who has drawn himself up very straight and is fumbling with his glasses.

'You could have *died*. In light of this, I have done a lot of thinking over the last few days. And not much sleeping, to tell you the truth.' He snorts a mirthless chuckle, but nobody joins in.

'So, I'll just say it. I've decided to resign as teacher on this project, and to be honest, I need time to re-evaluate whether I should carry on teaching at all. The company has already accepted my resignation and will advertise for a replacement as soon as possible. I'll remain here until that happens, probably for another month or so. It's the right thing to do.'

Zac and I exchange a glance. *Abandoning us at the height of the threat is the right thing to do?*

'What does that all mean?' whispers Struan to me.

'He's leaving. And he's not coming back.'

The rest of the morning is spent trying to focus on ratios and fractions. Outside, the sun shines and the trees sway in triumph. Whatever it is that's fighting us, it has struck another blow.

Ten minutes before break, I risk it. After all, Mr Johnston's news changes nothing. Not when you really think about it.

I scribble my secret note in as clear a hand-writing as I can muster and pass it below the table to Gregor. Each in turn, they look at their neighbour in surprise, rustle the note below the table, glance at me and pass it on. Minutes later, the bell rings and we push outside, silent and secret, like a conspiracy. Mr Johnston has turned straight to his marking. I beckon and they all follow round to the bench at the back. Zac has already checked that the windows of the school hut are closed.

'Right.' I check the faces one by one. Even Struan is listening, but of course he heard bits of it last night.

'Right,' I repeat, looking at Zac for reassurance.

Help! I have no idea what to say.

'Zac is now going to tell you all about our theory,' I say finally and sit down on the bench. He shoots me a furious look, but when he does begin, he explains it a thousand times better than I ever could.

'OK. Yes. Fine. So, you have probably noticed that a fair bit of stuff is going wrong for us here. Not just in school—on Skelsay. What's the worst thing that's happened, here, on the island?' He gives them a few seconds.

'Don't tell me what you're thinking of.' Zac waves down the couple of raised hands and I giggle; they, treat him like a teacher!

'The point is, it's a bit much, isn't it? Yeah? Well, Em and me; we think we've figured it out. When we came here to clear the land and build the resort, like the hotel and the golf course and the stuff that goes with it, we didn't consider what was here before. We are destroying the habitats—the homes—of all these plants and animals, and we're not really respecting the place. Pratt was all for bulldozing right over the bats, remember?'

More than one frown has appeared, but they are listening; puzzled, confused, but listening. That's better than I expected. I relax a little as Zac goes on.

'So, we wonder if what's happening means that nature, the wilderness, is fighting back. To get us all out of here, to get the island back.'

It takes a moment to settle in, but then I watch as our outrageous theory is *believed* rather than belittled. Their little faces are serious; they exchange glances, even a couple of nods, but then Zac resumes.

'We've tried to tell some of the adults. I've tried my parents, Em's spoken to her folks, and both of us have hassled Mr Johnston, but they don't believe us. I suppose it is hard to get your head round, even now.'

'But...' begins Anna.

Gregor completes her sentence for her. 'What do we do?'

'Fight back! Oh yeah! War!' Struan jumps up and

grabs a stick lying on the ground. He starts whacking a bunch of heather beneath his feet.

'Struan!' I hiss, kicking the stick out of his hand. 'Sit down! The thing is...'

All eyes are on me now. I'm not too sure how to say what I *know* to be true.

'The thing is...' I repeat. 'We need to get out of here.'

Zac steps forward, looking at each little face seriously. 'Em's right. We can't win this. Fact.'

CHAPTER TWENTY-SIX

FICTION

The mood is sombre as the afternoon's lessons begin. Mr Johnston would normally notice, but not today. He goes through the routine, but his heart isn't in it. It takes him being uninspiring and ordinary for me to realise how inspiring and extraordinary he has been all this time.

'I don't want him to go,' Struan mumbles as we walk home, the wind blowing the first loose leaves around our feet. Like Dad, he kicks stones at times like this and it is what he does now, swinging his leg right back and aiming for the water. Splash after splash.

My mind is on that stupid creative writing homework again. It feels like a lifetime ago that we complained about having to write so much. You'd think that almost dying might be excuse enough, but Mr Johnston wouldn't hear of it. Zac has done his, a kind of crime mystery. I wouldn't mind reading it, just to give me some ideas. *You need conflict*, Mr Johnston says, *it's the life-blood of a good tale.*

'Hey, Em, do you really, really believe what you said earlier?' Struan kicks another stone before glancing over. There is a small smile, hope rather than certainty. Hope that it's all going to be fine, that there's nothing to worry about. Hope that Zac and I are only kidding.

'I do believe it, Struan, and I reckon everybody will *have* to believe it when worse stuff happens.' I sigh. 'I'm just going to have to chip away at Mum and Dad. Mr Johnston was probably the one I was most hopeful about convincing, but now he's going…'

Struan says nothing, probably for the first time ever.

It is late the following afternoon when I finally sit down to tackle my story for homework.

'Em, I'm just going to take Izzy to the beach for a play before bed. Struan might come back from chanter lesson while I'm out. Are you going to be in?' Mum has pulled out the thick jumper from the chest; summer must be nearly over. Izzy is rattling the door. 'Izzy going to beach!'

'Yes, I'm not going anywhere, this story won't write itself.'

'All right. If it takes you longer than half an hour, you can have a couple of biscuits to keep your energy up. They're on the coffee shelf.'

'OK. Thanks,' I call absentmindedly.

I swing my legs, as if the motion could power my brain. *What's the point in fake conflict, between fake characters and fake powers?*

142

My eyes widen and there, at that moment, it strikes me. The very idea that could save us all.

If only I can get it right!

I straighten, reach for my pen and begin.

There was silence as the five family members unclipped their strained seatbelts and stretched their aching muscles. There it was, the ferry that would take them to their doom.

I must be related to Shakespeare! This is brilliant! Right, let's have a bit of dialogue now.

'I'm not sure about this island,' said Ellie, the oldest, to her new friend Jack. 'I have a bad feeling about this.'

At the very next moment, the children were attacked by a murderous mob of seagulls. The birds pecked and dive-bombed again and again, until Ellie and Jack fled below deck. Ellie, a very intelligent girl, began to suspect that something was seriously wrong, especially when stormy seas, freak weather and pests caused the building project many setbacks.

I lean back and admire my work. A quick count reveals I have already got more than a hundred words. This is going to be easier than I thought.

Mishap after mishap befell the small group of workers on the island, but the adults remained ignorant of the greatest danger of all: the fact that nature itself was against them. Terrible winter weather was followed by an invasion of rats stealing food and some near-fatal accidents. Ellie and her friend Jack attempted to warn the adults again and again.

'Please listen to us!' they begged their teacher, normally a reasonable man. 'Unless we leave now, we are going to die. No man is a match for this wilderness!'

The teacher, Mr Swanston, shook his head sadly. 'Ellie, Jack, I'm sorry—there is nothing I can do to help an over-active imagination. Let's drop this whole war idea, all right? After all, no reasonable person could believe in such a thing.'

Mr Swanston turned and stared out of the window.

I glance at the clock beside my bed: nearly seven o'clock. I heard Mum come back a couple of minutes ago, and Dad's humming as he nears the hut. Izzy must be too tired to shout.

Right, back to the task in hand. I have a feeling 700 words won't be enough. I read over the first part again. Not half bad. Maybe not the very best I've ever done, but some brilliant touches, no doubt about that. And there's no way Mr Johnston cannot get it, is there?

This next bit is going to be the crucial part. Setting

the scene a bit, maybe? Yeah, he'll like that.

The morning it all ended started like any other morning in the eight months the group had stayed on the island of Shellsay. The pink glow of sunrise illuminated the sky with streaks of purple, but dark clouds formed a giant monster's claw above the island as a flock of geese flew north overhead, disappearing behind the Ben with fading shrieks.

More clouds began to gather on the distant horizon, but each and every person went about their daily business as they had before. Darkness pulled over the island like a cloak, but unaware, the band of workers continued to dig, the group of children continued to learn, and life went by pretty much as it had. All of a sudden, a tremor shook the huts, just enough to make a full glass of juice spill...

'Dinner!' Dad's shout interrupts my thoughts, but I suppose I do need a break before throwing myself into the main event. Exhausted, I slouch next door to the kitchen. Throughout the meal I watch the story unfold in my imagination; I'd forgotten how much I like writing. Once you get over having to do it in the first place, it's all right. Fun, even.

Before bed, I set my alarm for 5.30am—I need an early start to finish my story before school.

Satisfied, I lay out my jotter and pen beside my bed. It's pretty convincing. For fiction.

I can only pray it makes a difference in real life.

CHAPTER TWENTY-SEVEN

DREAM

I wake, wheezing, as darkness presses in on me from all sides. The covers stick to me as I thrash to reach my clock and press the night-vision button. 03.34 am.

I switch my bedside lamp on and sit up, allowing my eyes to adjust back from the chaos of my imagination. My dream was so real: the thundering waves, the fury of the wind, screams, noise, running and fear.

That's what you get, I guess, for thinking about scary stories before bedtime. It takes a few more seconds for my breathing to return to normal. I turn the sodden pillow around, sink back and turn the light off again.

I toss to the right. My feet are too hot. The bedding feels damp round my neck.

I roll onto my left, but as soon as I close my eyes, the vision returns and I jolt upright. *Oh, it's no good!* Still shaking, I put the light back on and reach for my fleece.

I'm wide awake.

I grab my jotter and pen from the bedside table and

start where I'd left off. *Now, where was I?*

The wind began to whip the usually still water in the sheltered bay.

Everybody shrugged this off, putting it down to their overactive imaginations—everyone except Ellie who knew without a shadow of a doubt that the crucial moment had come. She ran to Jack's hut and rattled the door.

Some more dialogue, I reckon.

'Jack. Jack, be quick. It's coming: the final battle!' Ellie sank to the ground, exhausted by fear and worry.

Jack cast his eyes towards the sky and recognised the threat. 'If the danger is going to come from anywhere, it'll be the sea,' he said.

'Quickly! Everyone! Make for the highest point of the island. It's our only hope!'

My pen flies as I write of the horror vision I saw in my dreams. Dawn breaks, and still I write as if my life depended on it.

As if everyone's life depended on it.

By the time I finish, I must have written over a thousand words. Satisfied, I read the beginning again. Yes, this time he'll listen; they all will. They have to.

I close the jotter and place it in my schoolbag, ready to hand in.

The last hour of sleep is sweet and undisturbed.

'Em, this is substantial. I'm impressed.'

Mr Johnston scans the pages of my jotter, but I can tell he's not really reading. It's a teacher thing to do.

'And here is mine,' adds Zac, placing his own work on the teacher's desk.

'Wow, Zac and Em, whatever I've said about your laziness in the past, I take it all back. Writing at length is quite an advanced skill. Let's hope the quality is up to scratch, too. Why don't you go ahead and make a start on that ratio work and I'll begin marking these?' He trails off and saunters to the window, his hand with our jotters dropping limp by his side.

'I'll get the maths folder,' I volunteer, just because it takes me past the window. *Ah, I see.* There is a large boat at the pier and it looks like some of the roof constructions have arrived. Erica's crane is lifting them slowly over to the loading square.

'Don't dawdle, Em,' says Mr Johnston, even though he has just done exactly the same thing. *Teachers!*

By lunchtime, parts of the hotel begin to look like somewhere you could actually stay. As soon as the roof appears, even just in its skeleton form, it begins to feel real.

The little ones play *What's the Time Mr Wolf* without a worry in the world, even though they know.

To be fair, I am wobbling a bit, too—the wind is light, the air is fresh, the sun gilds every rock and tree. The project is coming on.

Mr Johnston rings the bell for the afternoon. 'All right now. Settle down.'

It always takes a minute or two, but eventually even Struan sits still and turns his face to the front.

'I was marking Em and Zac's stories over lunchtime, and I am particularly impressed by the vivid imagination in both. This is excellent storytelling, something you can all learn from as you write your own stories. Listen.'

I lose myself in the words, as if hearing it for the first time. Mr Johnston reads it almost how I imagined it and Zac laughs at all the bits about our family and even Struan's mouth hangs open, which is a sure sign he's absorbed in the story. There isn't a sound apart from Mr Johnston's voice and the gulls and distant shouts of the workmen fixing roof frames. He describes my vision with frightening clarity: how the wave is spotted in the distance, the frantic warnings ignored by all adults until it is almost too late, the final scramble up the hill, the exhaustion and fear.

There was no choice: if the adults wouldn't listen, the children would have to think for both. Ellie and Jack rounded up the children of Shellsay and urged them to run to high ground, the only place where they might have a tiny chance of survival.

The huge wave chased them, but their little legs ran and ran and ran. When they got to the top, they collapsed with exhaustion. Below them, the water level rose. Would the adults join them?

I shift uncomfortably in my wooden seat. Maybe I shouldn't have left it on a cliff-hanger. *Why is nobody talking?*

I get it. I thought the ending was a bit rushed myself, probably because I was so desperate to finish it, and so tired. Still, Mr Johnston could say "well done" or something.

'Right, Em, you've given us plenty to think about. Hasn't she, everyone?' He addresses the rest of the class. None of the other kids are smiling which must be because they know. Just that little thought is enough to make me cheer up a little.

'Thanks, Em, your natural storytelling ability is really coming through here—taking something that we recognise and turning it into something else altogether. Something...'

'Terrifying?' volunteers Zac.

'Something exciting and full of tension, I was going to say. Come on, Zac, you're not that easily scared.'

Johnston's eyebrows are raised high, but Zac doesn't answer. Instead, he holds our teacher's gaze, deadly serious and asks what I'm too afraid to ask myself.

'Mr Johnston, do you really not see it?'

'There is nothing real to see here, kids, just a story to imagine. I thought that, at your age, Zac, you'd be old enough to tell the difference. Anyway, back to the ratios now. Struan's group, you'll find your maths tasks on page 23. Zac and Em, yours is page 48 in the second book. Don't waste time now.'

'But you haven't even read Zac's story out!' I protest.

'You can get too much of a good thing. Maybe sometime tomorrow.'

'But that's a...'

'Don't argue, Em. The books are on your table, so there's no excuse. Page 48.'

The old Mr Johnston got irked sometimes, but now it seems to be his default setting.

'Best to leave it? For now?' I mumble and Zac agrees. He has that rare knack of getting all his work done, but every time I glance over he's got a faraway look, as if he's allowing his thoughts to swarm out and hover over the sea and the Ben and goodness knows where else.

'After school?'

'After school,' he whispers back.

I know better than to raise my head from my maths book for the next half hour.

Nevertheless, and despite my best efforts, I still haven't finished all the calculations by the time Mr Johnston tells us to pack up.

'Ahem… just before you go… the company has been in touch, and a possible successor has already been identified. That means I am likely to be leaving Skelsay in a couple of weeks' time. Sorry.'

He looks down and plays with the button of his thick cotton shirt. Struan and Mikey are counting down the seconds till the bell, oblivious to what he has just said.

Outside, Zac and I walk to the cove and sink into the sand as the little ones run home.

I feel utterly deflated. 'Johnston looks awful, doesn't he?'

Zac nods. 'Erica was round at Mum's for a coffee last night. She's pretty lousy, too. She'll miss him.' He pauses. 'Em, your story was good.'

I shake my head. 'It made no difference though. The question is: What's next, General?'

'Don't even joke about that, Em.'

'All right. Seriously then. What's next? What would have to happen for everyone to believe us?'

Zac rises and dusts the damp sand off his trousers. His hair blows in the wind like a warning flag.

'No idea,' he whispers and begins to walk back towards his hut where the kitchen light has just gone on.

CHAPTER TWENTY-EIGHT

VIGILANT

'Hey! Knock before you come into my room! I'm telling!'
Struan is already half off his seat when I stretch out my
arm to block his way.

'Stop. I need to talk to you.'

This makes him take notice all right. He is used to me
avoiding him, not seeking him out.

'Struan… what did you make of my story earlier?'

He hesitates. 'Good?' he volunteers.

'Did it make you think at all? About our war. With,
erm, nature?'

He nods.

'Look, Struan, I'm just asking you to keep your eyes
open. Be vigilant, you know.'

I turn to leave but Struan holds me back, his small
hand surprisingly gentle against my arm.

'What does vigilant mean?'

His head barely reaches my chest. His fingers are tiny
and cold as they creep around mine.

'Means pay attention. Watch out and don't miss anything. Get it?'

'I get it.' He leans into me for a moment and I ruffle his hair.

As soon as we emerge into the kitchen for dinner, we can tell something is different today. Dad is pouring fizzy juice.

'What's to celebrate?' I help myself before he can take it away again.

'Did you see the roof frames arrive?' He strokes his beard, and his eyes sparkle.

'We did.'

His deep voice rumbles with pride: 'Well, it's just that for the very first time since we got here, we are ahead of schedule! And the delegation from Prime Isles are coming the day after tomorrow, so the timing couldn't be better!'

He beams at us.

I wake up to the sound of my father's whistling. A quick glance at the alarm clock confirms it's already 7.30. When we lived in Glasgow I'd be up at this time, but here, thirty seconds' walk from school, that seems a bit excessive. I pull my duvet over my face for another precious few minutes.

What was that?

I rub sleep from my eyes and sit up with some difficulty.

There it is again, a small sound…

'Is that you, Struan?'

My door is slowly pushed open and my brother emerges. He closes it behind himself, gently.

Gently? This is Struan!

'What's up?' I ask as I swing myself out of bed and reach for my jumper.

'You're going to think I'm mad now. You are.'

'I think you're mad already! You're Struan; it goes without saying. What's up?'

'I'm just a bit worried…'

'Oh, for goodness' sake, Struan. What is it?'

In answer, my brother pulls back the thin curtain from my window to reveal a brilliant, colourful sunrise.

'And?'

'Just look, please. I'm probably wrong anyway.'

I stretch and yawn to get across how pointless I think this is and then focus my eyes at the horizon once more. There is a pink glow, reaching from one end of the horizon to the other. Towering clouds hang motionless, as if suspended from the heavens.

'Well spotted: it's morning. What now?'

'Look at the clouds, Em.'

'Clouds are clouds!' I pull the curtain. 'Are you going to leave so I can get dressed?'

'No. You told me to be vigilant.'

'Did I? Turns out I didn't mean it then. MUM, Struan

won't leave me alone!'

My brother pulls the curtain back with so much force that I think I hear it rip. 'LOOK at the clouds, Em!' he demands.

I open my mouth to shout, but nothing comes out as I finally see. The shapes are fuzzy, but unmistakeable. The massive claw, raised and poised to strike. Just as I imagined it.

Even as I take all of this in, a flock of geese crosses my vision from left to right, heading north past the Ben. I bite back a swear.

No. No no no.

Struan has seen them too. I can tell he remembers the geese in my story and it gives both of us a shiver.

My clothes feel heavy as lead as I put them on. *This can't be happening. It isn't happening. None of this is happening.* I keep chanting my mantra under my breath. The worst part is that Struan seems to look to me for some sort of guidance. I can't show him what to do, because I don't *know* what to do. *This can't be happening. It isn't happening. None of this is happening.* If I say it enough, maybe it'll make it true? *This can't be happening. It isn't happening...*

In a haze, I approach the breakfast table where Mum has taken over the whistling duties from Dad who is already out on the site.

'Cereal? Juice?' she hums, but I walk past her to the

little window in the kitchen.

'What are you looking at?' she asks, coming up and rubbing my shoulder from behind.

'Clouds.'

'Pretty this morning, aren't they?' She turns and busies herself with the breakfast dishes. 'Autumn is best for that, and for rainbows. Did you see the rainbow yesterday lunchtime? I'm going to have another go at a rainbow landscape one of these days, trouble is, they look cheesy as soon as you stick a rainbow in.'

I grunt my agreement, but squint at the clouds again. The sick knot at the bottom of my stomach unravels a little. No claw. The only shape I can see looks a little like a giant teapot.

'Em, come on. You're a bit slow this morning; look, Struan has already finished his porridge. Get a move on. I've squeezed some juice. Vitamins is what we need.'

She says it with a fake smile, like a TV advert.

'Are you OK, Em? You do look a bit peaky.'

About a million years too late, I giggle at her joke. Wrong call. She frowns at me and looks, really looks, right into my eyes. I stop breathing.

'What's up?'

It's the no-nonsense voice, the *don't-you-dare-give-me-any-crap* voice.

What am I going to say? I thought I saw a giant shape in the sky and I'm worried we're all going to die?

'I just feel a bit nervous, that's all.'

Understatement of the decade.

Her face relaxes into a smile. 'Ah you're not still on about that nature disaster thing! Em, you're twelve years old, nearly thirteen! Let's be reasonable, OK? Struan you're a bit quiet, too. What's wrong with your glass? Why are you staring at it?'

CHAPTER TWENTY-NINE

FEAR

'I don't think there's any point in worrying the others just yet, Struan. We're probably just a bit paranoid, and you know that clouds can pretty much look like anything. Just because you thought you saw...'

'*We* thought! You saw it too, Em and you were just as freaked out as I was!' He hurries towards the school hut and I follow at a run.

'All right, all right. Point is, nothing happened, nothing spilled, nothing so much as wobbled. We're OK.' I breathe deeply, but my shaky voice is far from disguised.

'Are you going to tell Zac?'

'Probably not.'

'Why?'

I grab his collar. 'Because I don't want to look like an idiot! You and me, we were being stupid this morning; don't you get it? Hey; what's that in your pocket?' I swear I saw his coat pocket move all by itself.

'Snarl. I'm taking him with me. Just in case. Look, there's Zac now!'

Struan doubles his pace.

'Struan, no way! Struan, I'll kill you myself if you… STRUAN! NO!'

My brother waves at Zac across the square. Outrunning me easily, he sprints right up to my friend and scuttles along beside him, lips moving ceaselessly. I groan and jog after him to limit the damage. As soon as I reach them, I burst into the conversation, talking far too loudly considering how out of breath I am.

'Don't listen to him, Zac, I'm just being paranoid. I only wondered for a moment, but then I realised…'

'Em, stop. Stop and breathe, right?'

Zac actually leans forward and steadies me with both arms.

'The truth is, I wondered, too. My window faces the same way, doesn't it? And I looked out and…'

'You saw it too?' The image of the cloud claws its way right into my stomach. It takes all my willpower not to double over.

'Yes. The geese flew across just before eight and it reminded me, and then I really looked at the clouds, but to be honest, I wasn't sure. I can see where you got the idea though, Struan.'

Struan has turned towards school where some of the younger ones are now gathering.

'Best not to say anything to them yet, buddy,' says Zac, offering his hand for a high five.

I bet Struan would have liked a big brother.

Zac begins to walk again. 'We'd better get to school. No excuse for being late in this place, is there?'

How can he smile like that, with all that's going on?

'Look, both of you, chances are it'll be OK. No point in panicking until we know what we're up against, is there? We just need to keep our eyes open.'

He winks runs ahead the last few steps towards the school hut, probably to give me a chance to pull myself together.

Which is easier said than done when today might be my last day on this earth.

Mr Johnston is already handing out science jotters when I finally slide onto my seat.

'Right, everyone, morning all. I thought we'd get this over and done with as soon as possible. Don't want you to be in limbo longer than necessary. As you know, next week will be my last here and when this Miss Sinclair gets here, I would like to have up to date assessments in place, so that she knows about everyone's strengths and weaknesses—I mean, next steps.'

Mr Johnston seems a little more animated, now that he has a new thing to focus on: torturing us for the remainder of his time here.

'What's he on about?' I whisper across to Anna as Zac

has turned his chair and is facing out of the window.

'Science test,' she replies. 'Remember?'

I do *not*, as it happens, remember a single word being said about a science test. A quick glance at Struan confirms that even he was expecting this. I hate being outdone by my brother! I sigh, reach into my bag for a pencil and pull the question paper towards me.

A few minutes later all is silent. Mr Johnston's chair creaks as he gets up to adjust the curtains. I narrow my eyes and re-read the question. *Why can't I remember any of this stuff?*

Struan's pencil is busy scoring the paper. His test must be easy—that's the only explanation. I keep glancing out of the window, but no more monsters—the shapes have merged together into a single, impenetrable sheet of grey. Again, Mr Johnston gets up, this time to switch the light on.

'Ten more minutes.' He sinks into his chair. It is the creak of that chair which stands out as my last clear memory before it happens.

CHAPTER THIRTY

LISTEN

I look up. I don't know why. I must have sensed something, I suppose.

The door flies open: the light flickers and goes out and somebody screams as the metal walls of the hut rattle and the door bangs shut. Mr Johnston's coffee cup slides across his desk towards me. He staggers up to stop it, but it spills right across my test paper. I hold on to my wobbling desk as all around me, display boards clatter to the ground, sheets of paper sail through the air, and chairs scrape across the shifting floor. A small crack has appeared on the window, just to the right from where Zac is sitting. He is holding on to his seat, teeth clenched and as we briefly catch each other's eye, a grim understanding passes between us.

Just as suddenly as it started, it stops. A breathless silence lingers, but it can only be a few seconds before we all start to stir, rubbing sore shins and turning around, dazed and bewildered.

'Stay where you are!' yells our teacher. As soon as he is out of the door, we follow. He is the adult. He should know what to do. He has sprinted down to the building site where the crane lies on its side, a smashed roof frame beside it, like match sticks.

The workforce gathers round. Dad is slamming his fists against the window of the crane. Both he and Mr Johnston reach in and help Erica climb out, carefully and slowly.

'All right?' Dad asks and she nods her head, shaking small pieces of glass from her clothes.

'Sorry, Will. I've no idea what happened there. Just lost control of it,' she manages to say. 'Are we insured for this?'

'Don't you worry about that. Don't worry at all. The main thing is that you're all right.'

'That was a sizeable tremor,' interjects Mr Johnston, rubbing Erica's back.

Everyone on the island is here, standing and watching.

I look around my family, my friends, the people I have grown to care about and there is no choice: I must speak up. Now. Struan's mouth is tight, his eyes fixed on me; he is waiting.

By now there is a steady murmur, spreading mouth to mouth. Little ones soothed by their parents, the instant high-pitched chatter of shared fear.

Zac gestures at me.

I clear my throat. 'Listen, everyone.'

Mum shakes her head at me, her eyes imploring me to stop. She is begging without words.

'LISTEN! PLEASE!' I begin.

Mr Johnston looks thoughtful, as if his brain is finally piecing it all together, but I can't wait for him to get it.

'You HAVE to listen to me if there is going to be any hope for us at all.' I dig my fingernails into my palms and the pain focuses my mind.

'We've tried to tell you this before, myself and Zac. The wilderness on this island is fighting us, fighting back against what we're doing here. It's a war, and this is the final battle. Our time on this island is up.'

Most of the faces are still serious, but the two brickies exchange a wry glance.

'I had a dream. A vision, I guess.'

A few more smiles are spreading. Mum has started elbowing her way through in my direction. I don't have much time left.

'And in that dream, all of this...'—I gesture at the chaos around me—'... all of this happened. The clouds this morning looked just like the ones in my story and now we've had the earthquake, just like in the dream, but...'

Mum has reached me and puts her arm around my shoulders. Despite the caring smile, she hisses into my ear: 'Stop, or so help me! You're freaking people out!'

I yank myself free. 'I WANT to freak them out! You all need to understand because you don't know what's coming next. We need to move, and quickly...'

Dad's booming voice carries over everyone and completely drowns me out.

'No need to panic. We are all unhurt. Petra is our first aider, as you know, so she can have a look at any minor issues. Erica, you should see her first.' Petra rushes off, probably to find her first aid kit. All the others wait for my father to continue.

'Everyone, later we'll clear the debris of this roof frame and see if we can salvage anything from it. Harvey, make a note to check for structural damage. There's a surveyor with the delegation due tomorrow, so he should be able to advise us. But for now, back to your huts, everyone, it looks like it's going to pour down any moment. Go! All good. Go!'

To my surprise, my father turns his back on me. His hand makes a waving gesture: *join the rest of them, go before I lose my rag at you.* Amazing, how eloquent a waving hand can be.

Zac has waited for me, and together we head back to the school hut. Mr Johnston kisses the back of Erica's head and follows us.

'It's a bit like your story, isn't it Em?' our teacher jokes, winking as he overtakes.

I picture the giant tidal wave, foaming and frothing

far out at sea, gathering height and speeding right towards us.

'How long do we have?' I ask Zac.

He shrugs, but for someone so laid back, he is agitated, looking back at his hut where his mum, Muriel, has just disappeared.

'Zac, I *know* this is real. They won't listen to me, but they might, just might, come anyway. It's our only chance.'

We enter the classroom just as Mr Johnston is striving to establish some sort of order. I do a quick head count, making sure all the kids are here.

'NOW!' I yell. 'Come on, everyone! To the Ben, no matter what anyone says. Right NOW!'

Just at the door, I turn to Mr Johnston whose speechless face is pale.

'Sorry, sir. Please come with us,' I plead. 'It's a sort of life and death thing.'

CHAPTER THIRTY-ONE

TIME

To my surprise, all the children follow me outside at once. Late morning feels more like dusk, with the tight roof of rainclouds over our heads. The wind has picked up even more and we run past the stunned group of adults, only slowing down to scream: 'Tidal wave, coming right for us! Everyone! Up the Ben! Quick!' Other children's voices join the chorus, shouting for mums, dads, urging and begging, but running—still running—up the steep slope to the woods.

The stampede of little feet behind me pushes me further, faster, for longer than I ever thought I could run.

Please let them come. Please make them come. Make them come; they've got to come...

I turn to check, but Zac, running beside me, shoves me onwards. Instead, he screams back over his shoulder at the stationary group of adults outside the school. 'COME ON!' His voice is already hoarse, but he pours all his desperation and worry into that shout.

I trip and narrowly avoid running into a birch tree. Some of the younger kids are slowing down, but they don't see what I see, my dream on endless replay in my mind: dirty brown waves carrying whole walls away with a single thrust; trees spliced and snapped by the sheer destructive power of the deep; mud and rocks, grinding all in their path to dust.

Inwardly, I am praying harder than I have ever prayed before. *Please, please, please let them come. Let them come: Mum and Dad and Izzy and all the others; oh let them come, let them come, let them come.*

The shouting has almost entirely subsided. Puffing, I push on, herding the wee ones higher and higher. Zac, Struan and Gregor are ahead of us, but only just. We reach the treeline; despite the daytime, the wood feels dark like the dead of night. I turn to the kids beside me: 'Keep going! Your parents *will* come after you. Push on, push on!'

We clear the trees and slash our way through the bracken until, finally, we reach the first clear view.

Turning, I just have time to take in Mr Johnston, half hobbling, half running behind us. I breathe deeply as I scan the horizon. Where will it come from?

The line between sea and sky looks fine, just a silver thread separating the sombre clouds and the murky sea. Normal. Just as it usually does.

'See anything?' I ask Zac as he scours the skyline with

his binoculars. He doesn't answer.

The silence is beginning to be awkward. *Did I get it wrong?*

But I don't need magnification to spot another threat: Mr Johnston is approaching at a walk. Even from here, I can see his flushed face, from running or rage, or maybe both.

'Anything?' I urge Zac. He lowers his binoculars and shakes his head. Our teacher is so close we can hear his feet crunch on the bracken.

'False alarm?' I ask, hopefully. Zac's eyes have that automatic look, machine-like, panning left and right and left and right.

'Maybe we need to get higher up, so we can get a better view?' he suggests, not taking his eyes off the sea. All the other kids stand around us, like sheep, waiting to be nipped at the heels and chased along.

Mr Johnston pushes himself up the last rocky outcrop to join us and doesn't waste any time.

'That's it! You will come back down with me, all of you. Now! In all my years of teaching, I have never— NEVER—come across defiance like this. You will regret this, especially you two!' His face is like a red balloon, about to burst.

He puffs and spits between sentences, but his voice loses none of its venom. I can actually see the veins pulsing in his temples.

I imagine what may lie in store for me when I return. The quiet disappointment of my parents, the sideways looks at Em the troublemaker, and Mr Johnston's handover chat with the next teacher: *Oh yes, Em. She needs watching, that one.*

'Over there! What is that?' Zac's voice slices into the thick silence. The wind howls in reply as Zac's hand stretches out and points northwards, right over the new hunting lodge at the hidden tip of the island, to something in the endless ocean.

Nope. I see nothing. Nothing unusual, anyway. Hang on.

My knuckles are white as I impatiently brush my hair aside.

Zac gives a low whistle. He lowers the binoculars to look at me and nods.

'It's coming,' he croaks.

Although it's what I expected, the reality rocks me to my core. Icy shivers run down my lower back, my arms, my neck. *A life and death thing. Fact.*

Now I can see it, even with my naked eye: the horizon has changed. The distinct line between sea and sky has smudged, obscured by a watery wall of angry froth which grows higher and wider with its advance; ready to wipe out the enemy once and for all.

Us.

We have no way to fight back. This is going to be a rout;

a massacre.

I'm hypnotised, as if the wave had already carried me away. I can't react to the children's chatter, or to Mr Johnston holding out his hand to receive the binoculars from Zac, or to my friend's frantic stabbing at his phone with his thumb.

Finally, something inside me snaps. *What on earth am I thinking? I don't have time for this. I don't have time at all.*

Before anyone can hold me back, I hurtle down the hill again, past Struan, past Anna, Gregor, Catriona and Mikey, past Erica and Petra who have obviously decided to follow us—maybe to see what the fuss is about. I hear my name, shouted but muted, like you hear underwater, but I run on. I make much, much faster headway than I did on the way up. I stumble over something but I scramble up and stagger on, with a sharp pain in my right ankle now. The trees are dense under the thick cloud cover. I pass Muriel rushing uphill but don't stop. A branch hits me on the side of the head so hard that I momentarily lose my balance. And then I hear them: low shouts, fragments of cries carried by the wind. I stop to listen.

'Roger... phone... tidal wave... see it now...' The shouter swears loudly. A man, that's all I can be sure of.

'Go... evacuate... Ben now... Hurry! Everyone...'

That second voice sounded like Dad. It sounded like

Dad! And if I can hear *him*…

'DAAAD! COME ON!' I scream so loudly that my lungs might burst. It doesn't sound a thing like me. 'MUUUM! WE'RE UP HERE! RUN! IT'S COMING. IT'S COMING RIGHT NOW!'

Hurtling through the trees again, I almost crash into Mum who is struggling to drag Izzy along. She stops and I hug her like I've not hugged her in years: fierce, and desperate, and hard. The skin on her face is clammy on mine.

'Go. Hurry, Mum, please. Please.'

She shakes her head.

'PLEASE. It won't be long before it hits. Izzy, you need to run fast for Mum.' My pulse is pounding. 'Where's Dad?'

'Still at the site.'

'Go. Go, go! See you up there.'

She hesitates but I push her in an upwards direction, shouting over my shoulder, 'I can run faster than you.'

I should have known. Dad's like the captain of the sinking ship. There is no way he is going to leave until he knows that the very last person is safe.

I'm going to watch my father die.

NO!

'COME ON DAD!'

He can't hear me.

I have reached the slope and see him in the distance,

waving his arms. Most of the workforce is scrambling up the Ben via the steep cliffs, shorter, quicker, yes, but much harder too.

The wave...

Once more, I'm near paralysed as I watch it smash towards us in slow motion, sucking all light out of our little settlement. Before it, Skelsay is nothing but a speck of dust, about to be swept away and discarded, and all of us with it. Already I can make out the arsenal of weapons the wave hides under its frothing coat—rocks and flotsam and tangled nets, enough sand to bury us all several times over.

Frantic, I try to think: *What will make my stubborn father move?*

Then I realise my only hope. And his.

Me.

'Dad, help me! HELP ME!' I hobble a little as I show myself to him. My ankle is throbbing and my shoe seems tight to bursting.

'OVER HERE! I'M HERE!' I shout.

He freezes.

Then he shoots towards me like a coiled spring. The wave is so close now; higher than three huts stacked on top of one another, as it casts its shadow over us both. Dad sprints towards me with giant strides. I turn to clamber up the slope ahead of him. My arm is nearly pulled from the socket as he grabs it and pulls me forward. 'What are you doing, Em? I thought you were...'

His words are washed out by the sudden roar of noise and the ground begins to vibrate beneath our feet. White-eyed, we race each other through the trees, cutting up the steepest parts, clawing onto saplings and heather as we haul ourselves up, up, up, on all fours.

Both of us are knocked clear off our feet as the wave's impact thunders onto the pier below us. We don't waste time to look.

Within seconds we are scrambling again. Up, up, only up! The crashing waters are now accompanied by sounds of clashing metal and I imagine our huts, batted about by the surge, smashed and pounded against each other. *Up, up, up; don't stop!*

Behind me, sturdy tree trunks are snapping like cocktail sticks. Dad is close. I can feel it. And that's all I need to know as I brace myself for impact.

The wave's roar is deafening; blinding darkness engulfs us. Our feet search and search for ground which dissolves all around us.

'HOLD ON! DAD, HOLD ON!'

Brine and mud hurls itself at me, petrifying me with its cold whip strikes. My jeans feel like lead armour—I move in slow motion now and cast about for the strongest tree I can reach. A few steps downhill, Dad is hanging onto a thick birch. His teeth are clenched, veins protruding from his forehead and neck with the effort.

I have to settle for where I am; holding on to whatever this sapling is. Reaching a thicker tree would mean letting go.

There is little I can do but resist the strength of the pull and the scraping of *goodness-knows-what* along my legs. The chill seeps from my submerged hips and legs right into my defeated heart. And Dad, is down there, somewhere below me in the gathering dark…

I expect the water to rise, to cover my shoulders, my neck and my head—to suck me under and swallow me like a sweet. Instead, the mud reaches barely to my thighs now. I lock my arms around my sapling which bends spinelessly whichever way the flow takes it—and me with it. Closing my eyes, I concentrate on one thing only: staying alive. *I must hold on. Breathe. Not let go.*

Has it been seconds or minutes or hours? I don't know.

When I begin to take in my surroundings once more, winded by the cold and gasping, I remember my father, I crane my neck towards his birch tree.

But he's gone.

CHAPTER THIRTY-TWO

SMOKE

If my watch still works right, it's about six o'clock when I finally come out of my stupor of grief. He is gone. Washed away, wrenched from his safety hold. Gone.

Only flashes of moonlight flit through the clouds. The sea-slime is barely up to my knees now, but I am not sure there is even any solid ground left beneath. Still, for Mum's sake, I have to try. Try or die.

I consider letting go and reaching for the nearest tree trunk still standing. It's just there, almost within touching distance. But it may as well be a mile away, unless I can find a foothold.

Snapping off the thickest branch I can manage, I use it to prod into the slime, propelling myself upwards. Strong currents still swirl around my legs, tugging at what's left of my jeans.

With each movement, the cold shock cuts through me again. I push myself forward with the broken branch in my right hand and hold on to anything that may steady me with my left.

Why is everything so slow; so very, very slow?

Eventually, I drag myself free from the swamp and stumble on, climbing up and up until I reach dry rock and bracken. Collapsing onto the grass, I fumble in my pocket for my phone—but there is no pocket anymore.

My trousers are torn; my phone is gone. And with it, my only way of communicating.

I crouch, painfully bending my bruised legs, and pull my fleece down as far as it will go. Reaching around me, I rip out heather and bracken and cover myself as thickly as I can. Soon, the rain starts to fall good and proper.

I lie back and the world goes as black as black can be.

I am woken by faraway voices and a vaguely familiar smell.

I push my aching body upright. The hilltop is deserted, windswept and majestic. A solitary deer, standing sentry, disappears from an outcrop above me.

What's that smell?

With a start, I scramble to my feet and look around, though the world spins at first.

Fire. It's smoke, of that I'm sure. Oddly, I'm quite resigned to waiting for death, whatever way it may come, but burning in some heath fire is a different thing altogether. Leaning heavily onto my branch, I close my eyes, take a deep breath, and try to move, my ripped trainers squelching with every step. My numb legs move like ghosts. Once my vision settles, it reveals a cloudy sky, much like it was on the day we arrived on Skelsay.

It's the view below that has changed beyond all recognition. Water churns around the treetops in the lower part of the woods.

The Skelsay that we knew is gone. And with it, everything that Dad built here.

Gone.

And then I remember: *Dad…*

Oh Dad.

I wobble once more but regain my balance and begin to move; if I'm going to live I'd better find shelter. It's a logical thought.

Half stumbling, half crawling, I follow the smoke.

Trudging through moorland and scraping over rocks, I plod on. I thought all my emotion was spent, but relief at seeing my siblings and mother with the others, gathered around a small fire at the entrance of a cave, engulfs me and I sob like a baby. I will always treasure the memory of that first human touch warming my frozen skin. Hot tears mingle with rain on my cheeks.

'Dad?' Mum mutters into my ear.

I shake my head and she nods, slowly. As far as I'm aware, that's the last thing she says to anyone that night.

To be honest, I only take part of it in. I zip up my

jacket and wrap myself up as tight as a caterpillar against the cave wall. Erica is tending the fire and someone has gathered blueberries or something a bit like it. Zac crouches beside me.

'Want some food?'

'No.'

'You OK?'

'No.'

There is a pause. He stares at me, kindly, but how can he know what if feels like? Both his parents are here: I can see both Muriel and Harvey, trying to make a makeshift washing line out of a belt, drying some of the youngest ones' clothes over the fire. Steam rises, so it's obviously working.

'Do you want me to leave you alone?' he says finally.

'Yep.' My voice sounds low and automatic.

I don't look up but I feel his eyes linger on me for a while before he pulls away and steps out into the rain. *I bet he was the one who had matches.* He was the one who believed it, all of it, right from the very start.

Without him I wouldn't have had the courage to flee, or to take anyone with me. Without him none of us would be here.

But I almost hate him for it.

I must have dozed off, for I'm woken by startled cries outside.

'Is it a rescue helicopter?' someone shouts hoarsely.

Another asks: 'You sure now?'

And then there are many, mingling in a desperate chorus: 'Give me that branch, NOW! HERE! OVER HERE! Grab another one and hold it in the fire, quick! Yes, and now wave it high. HERE! We're down HERE!'

I crawl to the mouth of the cave where Muriel and Mr Johnston are waving burning twigs in the air and jumping up and down. Now I hear it too; a chopper noise travelling on the damp air.

'They saw us—they're coming! They're coming for us,' Erica shouts. 'About time!'

I didn't even hear her creep up beside me. She crawls through into the back of the cave where Petra and Mum lie with the younger kids. Struan and Izzy are cuddled right into Mum's fleece and I suddenly feel very alone.

With a supreme effort of will, I raise myself upright, biting down hard on my lips to distract myself from the pain in every tiny part of my body.

It's darkening and overcast, but there is a helicopter. No, there are two! Another one is approaching in the distance, swinging round the southern tip of the island and heading for us. I look around. *Where will they land?* There isn't anywhere flat enough to land a chopper. The helipad *was* down there somewhere, covered by a murky expanse of water now.

By and by, we are joined by the rest and for the first time it occurs to me to take stock. All the children are here of course... I count fifteen adults, all looking haggard and drawn. *Who is missing, apart from the one I won't allow myself to think about?* I don't see one of the apprentices, or Rab, the brickie. Pretty much everyone else is here.

The very last of the daylight is draining away as a rope is let down from the hovering helicopter, and one by one, we are winched to safety. The youngest ones are first, followed by Mum and Petra and the rest of the kids. They try to persuade Muriel to go, but she shakes her head, anxiously peering into the darkness. I am so cold that I find it hard to process any thought at all.

I step into the harness being held out for me, as Mr Johnston pats my head. He means well, but I am not reassured.

My stomach plummets as I'm yanked off my feet and swung into the air, my bare legs dangling, pelted by rain. The winchman strapped in next to me talks in a low voice, but who can listen when the world has simply fallen away? I try not to look down, but I can't help it. All that is left of our settlement is a cluster of upturned faces by the fire.

Skelsay looks nothing like itself anymore. The shape is all wrong, with only foaming dark waves where there should be huts and buildings and vehicles and...

Hold on!

I twist my body so suddenly that my winchman swears.

Thank God! Oh, thank God...

I cannot get the words out, my mouth paralysed by the cold, but I know what I've seen.

As the helicopter swings away and heads east to the mainland, I watch the tiny image of three people in the distance, inching their way closer to the cave. Zac's blond mop on the left. Harvey's chunky frame on the right.

And in the middle: Dad's fluorescent vest.

CHAPTER THIRTY-THREE

LESSONS

'And now: breaking news from the Western Isles. A drama has been unfolding over the past few hours on the little-known Hebridean island of Skelsay. Following a tremor in the Atlantic Ocean, measuring 7.9 on the Richter scale, a twelve-metre tidal wave engulfed the island at around midday. The larger island of Harris, and nearby Taransay were affected to a lesser extent.

'Skelsay had been uninhabited for at least four hundred years, but for the last eight months, a small construction workforce has been based there to build a luxury holiday retreat.'

The newsreader clears his throat before proceeding. The map of the Hebrides behind him changes to a picture of the artist's impression—the one from Dad's desk.

'Due to the sudden and violent nature of the event and the lack of warning, it was feared that the number of fatalities among the workforce and their families would be high. However, in the early evening, and despite complete submersion of the inhabited part of Skelsay, the majority of flood victims were discovered alive and well. The rescue operation is set to continue throughout the night.'

The image of a single helicopter against dark clouds cuts to shots of spraying waves on rocks and finally to footage, taken from the chopper, showing Struan and a winchman at the end of the rope zooming towards the camera.

'Survivors were initially airlifted to Stornoway, where many have been kept in hospital for observation, and some are still receiving treatment for their injuries.'

The pictures show us huddled in blankets in the hospital lounge, being handed bowls of soup. I'm surprised the steam shows so clearly on telly. The newsreader's face is back, wearing its expression of studied concern and talking straight at the camera.

'We can now talk to our North of Scotland correspondent, Fergus McFadden, who is with project co-ordinator and chief construction engineer Will Shepherd in Inverness.'

'DAD, you're on now!' Struan shouts, stating the obvious. We are all watching together from our hospital room, where Struan and Izzy have made a sort-of pen with their legs on the hospital floor and are letting Snarl run around—while the nurses are out of the room, anyway.

Mum arrives back with coffee just in time to catch Dad's moment of fame.

'Thank you for talking to us today, Mr Shepherd, especially considering your own significant injuries. How are you feeling?'

'I feel OK, and very grateful,' answers the Dad-on-the-screen.

The interviewer nods. 'And can you tell us what happened?

Dad begins. His leg, in plaster and broken in several places, is raised and dominates the picture as he speaks at length of our ordeal. 'Nobody, of course, can foretell a freak event like this, but one thing's for sure: this experience has taught me a couple of important lessons.'

'Like what?' asks the interviewer.

'Like that we need to be very, very sure before we meddle with the natural world in a place as wild as Skelsay.'

The interviewer keeps his composure, although he looks sympathetic, as if Dad should be excused for losing his mind. But my father isn't finished yet.

'And that you ignore the instincts of children at your peril. I nearly paid with my life for that particular mistake.'

I twist in my hospital bed and glance at Dad in his. Both of us are probably too embarrassed to hold the eye contact, but I know what he means.

'Look, Em, I'm really...'

'It's OK, Dad.'

And it's true. I don't want his apology, not now and not ever. I can hear laughter from the room next door where Zac and his family are supposed to be resting, and even though it's really late, I can't help joining in, out of relief and gratefulness and I don't know what else.

POSTSCRIPT

FIVE YEARS LATER

My stomach stirs as we approach the shape of the monster, just as we did the February of the year I turned thirteen.

I scan the surface of the sea.

None. No seals at all.

I breathe deeply and allow the sunshine on my face to burn away my fears while the two men talk.

'I don't think we'll go ashore. What do you think, Harvey?'

'No, let's sail around it a bit. Just for a wee look.'

I'm happy to leave them to it. Zac is doing a good job steering and I can't believe how much he's changed. Off to leave home soon, just like me.

'Are you looking forward to going, Zac? To uni, I mean.'

'Of course!' he answers.

'Not nervous? Doing Marine Biology? After all that's happened?'

'No, not really. I actually thought the same with you and Creative Writing. It's not like that's without baggage either, is it?'

We both laugh.

Fumbling, I pull the crumpled piece of paper from my jacket pocket. The artist impression of the Skelsay Skies Resort. I still can't believe it survived all of it, right from the moment it blew out of *I-am-a-prat*'s hand. Creases line the paper like scars. I smooth it carefully, as I have done so many times over the years. I don't know why it's so important to me, but I need to do this right here. Of that I'm sure.

'Here goes.'

'Better hurry, Em. We need to get back for dinner. All the restaurants are going to be mobbed with the Mod. Is it tonight Struan's competing in that piping thing?'

'Yes! All right, all right.'

I study the paper, drinking in the image for the last time.

Then I glance up at Skelsay's wilderness, back like it was before we came. Like it should be.

Like we should have left it.

The trees sway. The water laps up at the rocks in the sunshine, and when I throw the crumpled memory into the water, it disappears without a trace.

THE END

AUTHOR'S NOTE

I can pin-point the precise moment the idea for *Wilderness Wars* came to me. Driving along a deserted coastal road on the west coast of Scotland on the way to a holiday cottage, something hit our windscreen, hard. There was no-one around: no other car whose tyres could have thrown up a pebble, no rockface from which a stone could have crumbled down.

Baffled, we looked around, but all we could see were gulls circling overhead. 'Bet that gull dropped a rock down on us,' I joked.

'Yeah, it doesn't want us to go to the cottage!' our daughter laughed from the back seat.

'The gulls say no!' my husband added in a preachy politician voice.

'*What if nature fights back?*' I scribbled into my notebook that night.

Of course a single idea is not enough for a book. Lucky, then, that I had so many other experiences to draw on. I was a volunteer for the RSPB Wildlife explorers, for example, a club which Zac would have loved! I have been divebombed by angry gulls, I have waded through raging torrents, I have wrangled with rodents. I did even once, see an eaglet in its eyrie. I am a teacher and enjoyed imagining how a classroom might work in an environment like Skelsay. All this, and more, fed *Wilderness Wars*.

But the key questions which underpin this book are to do with respect and restraint:

What right do we have to impose our will on the last remaining wild places? And who is held responsible for the damage we do?

Because, as Edward Abbey puts it, *'Wilderness is not a luxury but a necessity of the human spirit.'*

ACKNOWLEDGEMENTS

As always, my thanks must go to Anne Glennie of Cranachan Publishing for giving this book a chance, despite all the work it needed—just because I loved it so much.

Rob, Carla, Isla and Duncan—we have travelled many islands together and all my memories (many of them channelled into this book) are of you. I love you more than I can say.

Thanks to my friend Sandra for her unwavering support and constant encouragement, and to Alasdair MacArthur for unwittingly giving this book its first proper edit. I am also deeply grateful to Ross Wiseman and Isla Ferguson for their work on the book trailer.

Thanks to the eagle-eyed John Fulton who has helped me avert many a punctuation embarrassment, to Olivia Levez (author of *The Island* and *The Circus*) for the wonderful cover quote and to Scottish Natural Heritage for providing helpful information about procedure and bat conservation.

Thanks also to my go-to construction expert Kate Morris (I didn't have a clue!).

Over the years, I have really appreciated vital organisations like the RSPB and the National Trust for Scotland who continue to foster a love of wild places in me and so many others.

Finally, who could fail to appreciate the stunning Scottish landscape in places like the Hebrides, a constant inspiration to me as I travel and see more of it.

God's earth is precious.

We must take much better care of it.

ABOUT THE AUTHOR

Inverness-based Barbara
Henderson is the author of
historical novels *Fir for Luck* and
Punch. Her energetic school visits
are increasingly taking her across
the length and breadth of Scotland,
and sometimes beyond. As a

Drama teacher, she loves to get young people on their
feet as they respond to stories.

'Writing is like magic,' she says. 'I see something
in my imagination, and I try to capture it by writing
it down—nothing more than black marks on white
paper. Much later, young people see these black marks
on white paper and suddenly they see something too,
feel something of their own. I cannot think of anything
more special than that.'

Barbara shares her home with three teenage
children, one long-suffering husband and a scruffy
Schnauzer. Her garden always ends up a wilderness,
however hard she tries.

Find out more about Barbara and her writing
at www.barbarahenderson.co.uk and follow her on
Twitter @scattyscribbler and Facebook.

YOU MIGHT ALSO ENJOY...

The Beast on the Broch
by John K. Fulton
Scotland, 799 AD. Talorca befriends a strange Pictish
beast; together, they fight off Viking raiders.

Charlie's Promise
by Annemarie Allan
A frightened refugee arrives in Scotland on the
brink of WW2 and needs Charlie's help.

Fir for Luck
by Barbara Henderson
The heart-wrenching tale of a girl's courage to save her
village from the Highland Clearances.

A Pattern of Secrets
by Lindsay Littleson
Jim must save his brother from the Poor House in
this gripping Victorian mystery.

Punch
by Barbara Henderson
Runaway Phin's journey across Victorian Scotland with
an escaped prisoner and a dancing bear.

The Revenge of Tirpitz
by M. L. Sloan
The thrilling WW2 story of a boy's role in the sinking
of the warship Tirpitz.